BACK IN THE GAME

CRAIG HOPPER

Also by Craig Hopper

THE INSURANCE MAN
A tale of despair, friendship and love

Cover Design: Craig Hopper

ACKNOWLEDGMENTS

Thank you to my initial readers Lesley, Hayley, John and Rob for your time, feedback and suggestions. Your help is very much appreciated.

Also, thank you to Lauren for final proof reading and another great job with editing.

If you die and I live, I don't have a future. You are my life and I will always love you.

PROLOGUE

Belfast, Northern Ireland – Wednesday 8th April 2009

Another burst of bullets slammed into the bourbon casks and splinters flew into the air.

Crosby crouched even smaller behind the casks and swore through gritted teeth as he touched where a bullet had grazed the top of his right arm. He looked at the warm blood on his fingers and he swore again. He wiped his fingers on his jeans and he slammed a new magazine into the Walther PPS semi-automatic hand gun. He took a deep breath, counted to three, sprung up from behind the casks and let off four shots, screaming at the same time.

He was answered with another hail of bullets and more splinters from the casks flew up into the air.

The sobbing teenage girl behind the empty wooden crates to Crosby's right, screamed and tried to curl up into a tighter ball on the dirty warehouse floor. She continued her sobbing and screaming.

Crosby glanced at the girl and growled. "Fuck!" Another hail of bullets slammed into the casks and he crouched as low as he could behind them. The pain from the bullet graze was screaming at him and it was becoming more difficult for him to raise his arm to let off some shots. Blood was trickling down his arm and dripping off his index finger to mix with the dirt on the floor.

Crosby looked to his right at Rosie. She was lying on her back with her right hand over the two bullet wounds in her chest. Her white cotton blouse was soaked crimson and her blood was black in the dirt as it spread across the concrete floor towards him. She was bleeding out quickly and he could see the life in her pale blue eyes ebbing away. Tears welled up in his eyes and he shouted "ROSIE, HOLD ON. YOU'RE GOING TO BE OKAY."

She slowly stretched out her left arm towards him and the pain from the effort showed on her face.

"PLEASE GOD. PLEASE HOLD ON, ROSIE."

She managed a faint smile and blood bubbled up in her mouth. With one last effort she forced another faint smile, mouthed silently "I love you" and closed her eyes.

Crosby screamed "NOOOOOO! ROSIE, HOLD ON. PLEASE HOLD ON" and tears flowed down his cheeks. His body began shaking and he felt sick.

Rosie was still. She was gone.

Another hail of bullets slammed into the bourbon casks and more splinters flew over Crosby's head.

The young girl behind the wooden crates screamed again. She looked over at Crosby, her eyes pleading, *make it stop, please make it stop.*

Crosby took a deep breath, summoned up all his remaining strength and screamed like a banshee as he sprung up from behind the casks. He let off two shots just before two bullets slammed into his chest.

The girl was still screaming and sobbing.

Crosby cried out in pain and dropped the gun as he fell to the floor. He thought he heard sirens and the screech of tyres, and then the world went black.

Longhougton, Northumberland – 6:00pm Friday 1st November 2013

The battered pick-up truck stopped at the kerb outside of the church and the driver turned to his passenger. "This is as far as I'm going."

The shaven headed man just sat and stared out through the windscreen. Loud rock music thumped through the ear buds in his ears. He had not uttered a word, other than saying, "I'm going to Howick. The old rectory," when he was first picked up.

The driver scratched at his two day old stubble and tried again, this time raising his voice. "I said, this is as far as I'm going mister."

The man took an ear bud out of his right ear and nodded. He reached down and picked up the small, dirty, black back-pack from between his feet in the foot-well. He noticed how well worn and tatty his boots were and the corners of his mouth turned upwards into a slight smile. They had served him well in Afghanistan.

The driver leaned on the steering wheel and pointed at the windscreen. "Follow the road North through the village and where it forks, go right. Keep following the road until you get to a T-junction. Go right there, follow the road and then take the first lane you see on your left. Follow the lane and the first driveway on your right will take you up to the old Howick rectory." The instructions were said quickly. The man had made him nervous from the moment he had picked him up on the A1 heading north and he now wanted him out of his truck.

The shaven headed man grunted and nodded. He opened the door and climbed out into the dark, cold and damp night air. He slammed the door shut without looking at the driver and without a word of thanks for the ride. The cold north wind hit him and he shivered.

The pick-up truck driver breathed a sigh of relief that the scruffy, shaven headed man had gotten out of his truck. He put the pick-up truck into drive, released the hand brake and pressed down hard on the accelerator, just a couple of seconds after the front passenger side door slammed shut.

The shaven headed man watched the pick-up truck speed away from the kerb and turn right and out of sight a few seconds later. He sighed and looked up at the overcast night sky as light rain began to fall. He pulled the hood of his old, dirty parka up over his head, slung the back-pack over his shoulders and pushed his hands deep into the parka's pockets.

As instructed by the pick-up truck driver, he began walking North through the village, with the cold north wind blowing into his face.

The Old Rectory, Howick, Nothumberland - 7:30pm Friday 1st November

Robert Grant shot a look across the study at his wife, Anna, as the knocking on the front door continued to get louder. "We're not expecting anyone tonight, are we?"

She shook her head, put the oversized glass of red wine down on the glass topped coffee table in front of her, and got up from the old, soft, leather sofa to answer the door.

Two minutes later, Anna had still not returned to the study.

Grant looked up from his laptop and towards the study door. "WHO'S AT THE DOOR DARLING?"

There was no answer.

"ANNA! WHO IS IT? WHO'S AT THE BLOODY DOOR AND WHAT DO THEY WANT?"

There was still no answer.

Grant sighed loudly, balanced the laptop on the arm of the old, high backed leather chair, pushed himself up onto his feet and went to see what was happening at the front door.

As he turned right out of the study, he stopped dead in his tracks. The door was wide open, and Anna was standing with her left hand over her mouth. What little colour she usually had in her cheeks, had drained away.

The man standing in the doorway was soaked from the rain, which was lashing down. His jeans were dirty and had holes in the knees, and his boots were well worn and muddy.

Anna turned and looked at her husband.

Robert studied the man's face. He had hollow cheeks and his dark brown eyes were sunk back in their sockets. The corners of his mouth were turned upwards into the faintest of smiles. He was looking at a gaunt, mirror image of himself.

He smiled reassuringly at his wife. "It's okay darling." He then turned to the man standing in the doorway. "William. What are you doing here?"

His twin brother pulled down the parka hood and the faint smile spread wider across his face. "May I come in out of the rain?"

Robert nodded. "Of course. Come in."

William stepped through the doorway, stamped his muddy boots on the thick, course, door mat and smiled at Anna. He stooped and kissed her softly on the cheek.

Anna touched her face where William's stubble had brushed against her cheek, forced a smile back and closed the door behind him.

There were a couple of minute's silence in the hallway as the three of them stood and looked at each other. Anna broke the awkward silence. "I'll show you up to the guest room while Robert pours you a brandy to warm you through."

William nodded at his brother, followed Anna up the stairs, to the right and down the landing to the last door on the left.

Anna opened the bedroom door but did not go in. "You'll be comfortable in here. There's towels in the en-suite. You smell, take a shower."

William stepped into the bedroom and turned on the light. He turned back to Anna and smiled. "Thank you."

She did not respond, she just turned and walked away down the landing.

William closed the bedroom door when he heard Anna's footsteps going down the stairs.

Anna went back into the study and found her husband standing at the drinks cabinet. She watched him pour brandy into a crystal glass and then pour a large measure of 12 year old Glen Moray single malt whisky into an identical crystal glass. He drained the whisky in one mouthful.

Anna folded her arms. "Why is he here, Robert?"

Robert half turned from the drinks cabinet and shrugged his shoulders. He poured himself another large measure of whisky and drained it again in one mouthful. The warmth of two glasses of whisky in quick succession burned his throat and he said quietly, "We'll find out soon enough, Anna. Soon enough."

1:00am Saturday 2ⁿᵈ November

Robert Grant heard a creak on the stairs and suddenly became alert. He listened to the footsteps for a moment, gently pulled back the duvet, slowly swung his legs out of bed and slipped his feet into his leather slippers. He turned and looked at his wife, she was fast asleep. He stood up, took five steps and grabbed the old grey hoodie from the back of the rocking chair in the corner of the room. He quickly pulled it on over his head and tip toed quietly onto the landing. He stopped, listened and heard the front door close. He crept towards the stairs as he pushed his arms into the sleeves.

William Grant stepped out into the dark, freezing cold night. The wind was howling down from the north. He looked up at the sky and could not see any stars because of the thick cloud cover which threatened snowfall. He shivered as another gust of the icy wind hit him. He switched on the small torch in his hand and walked down the three front steps.

Robert crept down the stairs. At the coat stand he kicked off his slippers and pulled on his wellington boots. He stepped over to the front door, counted quickly to ten in his head and opened it. He stepped outside and closed the door quietly behind him. He listened for a couple of seconds and just barely through the howling gale, he heard footsteps in the gravel off to his left. He quickly walked down the steps and followed the faint sound of the footsteps.

William quickly walked across the field behind the house, following the small beam of light shining just a couple of metres ahead of him. He suddenly stopped and strained to listen through the gusts of wind for any sound of being followed. He just barely heard the sound of someone scrambling over the dry stone wall and then swearing. He smiled and began walking quickly, following the small beam of light.

Robert stepped onto the coastal footpath and saw the silhouette of his brother, looking out at the raging North Sea.

The roar of the sea crashing against the rocks at the foot of the cliff got louder as he got closer to his brother. He shouted, from about ten feet away, "WILLIAM. WHAT ARE YOU DOING OUT HERE AT THIS TIME OF NIGHT? IT'S FREEZING COLD. COME ON, LET'S GO BACK TO THE HOUSE."

Without turning around, William shouted back, "COULDN'T SLEEP."

Robert now stood just behind William's left shoulder. He shivered and tucked his hands under his arm pits. "Why not?"

William turned his head slightly to his left. "I couldn't stop thinking about Anna."

3:30am Saturday 2nd November

Anna turned over in bed and sleepily asked, "Where have you been?" as her husband pulled the duvet up to his chin.

He lied. "I couldn't sleep, so I made some hot milk and read for a while. Go back to sleep darling."

Anna turned over again and did not say another word.

9:00am Saturday 2nd November

Anna stood quietly in the kitchen doorway, watching her husband cook breakfast on the range. She had never seen him cook breakfast before, but he had insisted. She watched in silence for a few seconds more and said "I've just popped my head around the guest room door, to tell William that breakfast is nearly ready, and he's gone. The bed looks like it has not been slept in."

Her husband shrugged and did not look at her as he turned the sausages in the frying pan. "Well, I guess that's William for you. Here today, gone tomorrow"

"I guess so" and she turned and went into the breakfast room.

Newcastle upon Tyne - 10:00am Monday 6th January 2014

The banker stood up behind his desk, buttoned his suit jacket, smiled and held out his right hand for a handshake. "It's always a pleasure to see you Mr. Grant."

Grant returned the smile and shook the offered hand firmly. "It's nice to see you again Mr. Penworthy."

The banker unbuttoned his suit jacket, sat down and pointed to the black, leather high backed chair slightly to the left of his desk. "Please take a seat Mr. Grant."

Grant unbuttoned his heavy, wool top coat and his suit jacket, sat down and smiled.

The banker leaned back in his soft, black, leather swivel chair and smiled. "What can I do for you today, Mr. Grant?"

Grant crossed his right leg over his left and returned the smile "I'm thinking of setting up a small internet business from home, something to keep me occupied, and I want to transfer funds into this new bank account." He handed the banker a small, piece of paper with a bank account number neatly written on it in black ink.

The banker leaned forward across the desk and

took the slip of paper. He looked at the number and did not recognise its configuration. He put the piece of paper down on the desk and again leaned back in his chair. "This is not one of our account numbers."

"Correct."

"A foreign account?"

Grant ignored the question. "I want complete separation between my personal account and the new business account."

The banker nodded. "I see. How much is to be transferred?"

"Three hundred thousand pounds. Within the hour, please."

"That's a lot of money to set up a small home internet business."

Grant ignored the banker's comment. "I'd be grateful if you would oblige, Mr. Penworthy."

There was a long moment's silence and realising that Grant was not going to offer an explanation, the banker nodded. "I'll see to it personally, right now" and his fingers danced over the keyboard in front of him.

Two minutes later, the banker took a sheet of A4 paper from the printer beside his desk and handed it to Grant. "Confirmation that the transaction is complete."

Grant reached across the desk, took the sheet of paper and glanced at it. He smiled and rose from his chair. He folded the sheet of paper, put it into the left inside pocket of his suit jacket, and then buttoned the jacket and topcoat. He was still smiling as he offered his right hand for a handshake. "Thank you, Mr. Penworthy."

The banker stood behind the desk and buttoned his suit jacket. He nodded and shook the offered hand firmly. "As always, it's a pleasure to have been of service Mr. Grant."

Grant nodded, turned and left the office.

Brightside Insurance, Chancery Lane, London – 2:00pm Wednesday 6th May 2015

The conference room on the third floor of Brightside International Investigations was stiflingly hot. The edges of the uneaten sandwiches on the foil platters in the middle of the oval conference table, were starting to curl and the bottles of water were no longer cold.

Beads of sweat started to run down Bill Pike's face. He tugged at the skinny, grey, silk tie and unfastened the top button of his white, button down collar shirt. He was bored and not really listening to the conversation which was taking place around the table. He was so bored, that he started to take an interest in the L S Lowry reproduction on the wall opposite him. It was a legacy from Joe Crosby's time at the company. He studied the picture and decided that he did not like it. All he saw was matchstick men in flat caps, and matchstick cats and dogs. He made a mental note to buy some new art for the office walls.

"Bill. Are you with us?" The bald Office Manager asked in a booming west country accent.

Pike broke his attention away from the painting and looked around the table at the faces staring at him. His eyes narrowed, and his brow furrowed, as he wrote *JOE CROSBY* in black ink on the yellow notepad in front of him. He put the top on his silver fountain pen and put it down on the table next to the notepad. He stared at the name he had written on the page.

The fat man sitting next to him put his hand on his shoulder and gently shook it, "Bill?"

Pike looked up from the pad and quietly said, "Crosby."

The Office Manager was surprised to hear the name and coughed as he took a sip of the warm water. "What? Did you just mention Joe Crosby? Why bring him up?" He coughed again.

Pike looked up from the notepad and around the table. "If anyone can find Lord Grant's missing son, it's Joe Crosby."

"I heard he was dead," the fat man sitting next to Pike said.

The Office Manager shook his head. "You can't be serious, Bill."

The young investigator, the rising star in the firm, sitting opposite Pike, looked at the faces around the table. "Who's Joe Crosby?"

Pike picked up his pen and tapped the pad with it. "Joe could find William Grant, I'm certain of it."

The fat man leaned back in his chair and crossed his arms across his wide chest. "He probably could, but in case you haven't noticed, Bill, Crosby's been missing since he kicked the shit out of you at the Christmas party in 2009."

The young investigator's interest was really peaked now, and he asked again "Who's Joe Crosby?"

The Office Manager leaned forward on his elbows on the table. "Crosby's been out of the game for five years. What makes you think he would want to come back, after what happened in Belfast?"

The young investigator was now angry at being ignored and he slammed his cheap ballpoint pen down on the yellow notepad in front of him. "What happened in Belfast?"

The fat man glared across the table at him. "Fucking shut up. The adults are talking."

The young investigator's face reddened, and he slumped in his chair, crossed his arms and looked down at the table.

The fat man still glared at him and satisfied that the young upstart had been put in his place, he said "Now, where were we?"

"Joe could find William Grant. I'm sure of it." Pike said assertively.

The fat man said again, "I heard he was dead."

Pike sighed and shook his head. "He's not dead."

"Do you know where he is?" the Office Manager asked.

Pike shook his head again. "No, but I know someone who will know where he is."

The Office Manager spread his arms. "Who?"

"His sister."

The fat man started laughing and when he stopped, he said, "Good luck with that."

2:20pm Wednesday 6ᵗʰ May

Pike closed his office door and headed straight to the drinks cabinet. He poured himself a large bourbon and downed it in one mouthful. He felt the warmth of the liquor in the back of his throat, closed his eyes and bowed his head. "Fuck," he said loudly to the empty room and wondered why he had mentioned Joe Crosby.

The office door opened without a knock and the fat man walked in. "You've started early, Bill."

Pike turned. "I'm starting to regret bringing up Crosby. What do you want Ken?"

The fat man grinned. "Can I join you?"

Pike poured himself another large bourbon. "Help yourself."

The fat man closed the office door behind him and walked over to the drinks cabinet.

Pike sat in the soft, red, leather swivel chair behind his antique mahogany desk, and he turned and looked out of the window at the City of London skyline.

The fat man poured himself a large bourbon. He walked over to the red leather sofa against the wall, unbuttoned his suit jacket with his free hand and flopped his large frame down into it. He took a large mouthful of bourbon, looked around the office and nodded approvingly at the new décor. "I like what you've done with your office."

Pike continued to look out over the city. "Fuck off Ken. You didn't just come in here to admire the paintings on my office wall or just to drink my bourbon."

The fat man smiled to himself. "It is nice bourbon, by the way."

Pike turned away from the view out of his office window. "What do you want, Ken?"

The fat man took another mouthful of bourbon and savoured the warmth in the back of his throat. "Actually Bill, I did think that Crosby was dead."

Pike put his glass down on the desk and sighed. "He's not dead."

The fat man drained his glass. "Do you really want to bring Joe Crosby back into the business? Especially after what happened to Rosie and then between you both at the Christmas party?"

Pike sighed, picked up his glass, drained it and put it down onto the black leather writing mat in front of him. He slouched back into his chair and put his legs up across the corner of the desk. "For eighteen months, we've had all our investigators searching for William Grant and nothing, zilch. He's still missing." He felt a headache coming on and he gently started massaging his temples. He continued "You know as well as I do, that Joe Crosby was the best Finder in the business and if anyone can find this man, it's him."

The fat man downed the remainder of the bourbon in his glass and put the empty glass on the sofa arm. "That's nice bourbon, Bill."

Pike ignored the comment.

The fat man heaved his large frame up from the sofa and buttoned his suit jacket. He watched Pike massage his temples for a few seconds, "I hope you know what you're doing, Bill?"

Pike stopped massaging his temples and looked up. "I do, Ken. Joe Crosby can find this man."

The fat man nodded towards the empty glass on the sofa arm. "Thanks for the drink."

Pike swung his chair back around to the city skyline as the fat man left his office.

The young investigator looked up from his laptop as the fat man left Pike's office. He waited until the man was behind his own closed office door, then rose from his chair and walked around his desk to a bald, spectacled, investigator who was angrily clicking his pen. "Tom. Who's Joe Crosby?"

The pen clicking abruptly stopped and the investigator looked up at the young, handsome face. He leaned back in his chair and clicked his pen once. "Bloody hell. Joe Crosby. I've not heard that name in years."

"Who's Joe Crosby, Tom?"

The investigator was lost in the past. "Joe Crosby. Bloody hell, there's a blast from the past."

"TOM!" The young investigator quickly looked around the open plan office to see if he had just attracted unwanted attention.

"Oh. Sorry. He was the best Finder in the business. He got out of the game when his partner was killed in a gun fight in Belfast. He took two bullets in the chest and barely survived."

Before the young investigator could ask another question, the furious pen clicking started again and the bald investigator turned his attention back to his laptop screen.

The young investigator grunted and shook his head. He returned to his desk, typed 'Joe Crosby' into the company database search engine and pressed the return key. He clasped his hands behind his head, leaned back in his chair and watched the results appear on the laptop screen.

3:00pm Wednesday 6th May

Pike fastened the middle button of his suit jacket, picked up his laptop bag and left his office. He stopped at his secretary's desk just outside of the door.

The secretary looked up and smiled. "Leaving for the day, Mr. Pike?"

Pike did not return the smile. "Kelly, book me a single train ticket from Kings Cross to Doncaster, to leave tonight. Text me the departure time and I'll pick the ticket up at the station." He began walking away and then suddenly stopped. He turned back to the secretary. "Oh! And Kelly, hire me a car to pick up at Doncaster."

The secretary looked up from scribbling on the yellow notepad. "Okay, Mr. Pike."

"One more thing, Kelly."

"Yes, Mr. Pike?"

"Cancel all my appointments for the next seven days."

The secretary stopped smiling. "If you're cancelling appointments with clients, it must be serious. Is everything okay?"

Pike sighed. "It is serious. I'm going to find Joe Crosby."

The secretary's jaw dropped and all she could manage in response was, "Oh!"

Pike turned and walked away without saying another word.

The young investigator had overheard the conversation between Pike and his secretary and a couple of minutes later, when he was sure that Pike had left the office, he wandered over to the secretary's desk. He sat on the edge of her desk "Hi Kelly. Got anything nice planned for tonight?"

The secretary did not look up from her laptop. "Not with you, Lee."

"That's harsh, Kelly."

The secretary looked up and snapped, "What do you want Lee?"

"Why is everyone freaking out over this Joe Crosby?"

"Get lost, Lee, and mind your own business."

"Seriously, Kelly, who's Joe Crosby? The database literally says nothing about him."

The secretary sighed. "If I tell you, will you leave me alone?"

"Yes."

"Joe Crosby was the founder of this firm with Mr. Pike. They had been best friends since school. Joe's favourite saying was 'look on the bright side,' which is where the firm gets its name from."

The young investigator stood up and put his hands into his suit trouser pockets. "Why haven't I heard his name mentioned in the two years I've worked here?"

"Lee, go away. I've got work to get on with."

The young investigator shook his head "No. Not until you give me some more information on this guy."

The secretary sighed loudly. "Okay, this is the last thing I'm telling you."

The young investigator nodded.

"Joe was on a job in Belfast with his partner, Rosie Swan. It went badly wrong, Rosie got killed and Joe got badly hurt. He nearly died. He blamed Mr. Pike for Rosie's death and when he had recovered from his injuries, he came into the office during the Christmas party and kicked the shit out of Mr. Pike. Joe then vanished, and nobody has seen him or heard from him since."

The young investigator was about to ask another question, but the secretary cut him off. "Now get lost Lee. I've work to do," and she turned her attention back to her laptop screen.

The young investigator hovered at the secretary's desk for a few seconds, digesting the information he had just learned and then went back to his desk, still wanting to know more about Joe Crosby.

Doncaster station – 8:30pm Wednesday 6th May

Bill Pike smiled at the young, pretty car hire attendant and said, "Thanks," as he took the car keys from her.

She smiled back. "You're welcome Mr. Pike. Your car is out front and thank you for choosing to hire from GBR."

Pike nodded and said, "Thanks," again. He picked up his suit bag and slung it over his shoulder, grabbed hold of the handle of his small, travel light suitcase and went outside to the waiting Audi.

He threw the suitcase and suit bag into the boot of the car and slammed the lid shut. He walked around to the driver's door, opened it, got in and turned on the engine. The car purred quietly as he fastened the seatbelt. He pressed down on the brake, selected 'drive,' released the handbrake and drove the car carefully out of the car rental compound and onto the main road.

As Pike drove towards the M18 motorway, a knot was growing in his stomach. He was not looking forward to returning home to Rotherham. He turned on the radio to try and take his mind off it. The Rolling Stones.

House boy knows that he's doin' all right

You should have heard him just around midnight
Brown Sugar, how come you taste so good
Brown Sugar, just like a young girl should....

Pike nodded his satisfaction to the song. He started tapping his fingers on the steering wheel and sang along.

The Chorlton Hotel, Rotherham, South Yorkshire – 9:30pm Wednesday 6th May

Bill Pike opened the door to room twenty-one, stepped through the doorway and switched on the lights. The door swung closed behind him. He took two steps into the room and took in the scene. The décor was bland and boring, beige walls, beige carpet, a neutral colour duvet and the obligatory watercolour print on the wall. He sighed and shook his head.

He was tired, he had a headache and he did not like the room. He walked over to the bed, dropped his suit bag onto it and sat down. He looked around the room again, and decided he needed a drink. He sighed again, stood up, left the room with the lights still on and went to find the hotel bar.

9:35pm Wednesday 6th May

"A pint of bitter, please."

The barman nodded at the pumps in front of him, "John Smiths or Worthington's?"

"Worthington's."

The barman nodded, got a glass off the shelf and started to pull a pint of Worthington's."

Pike watched the pint being pulled and licked his lips.

The barman put the pint of beer down on the bar in front of him.

Pike picked up the glass "Charge it to room twenty-one." He took a long drink, put the glass down on the bar and wiped his mouth with the back of his right hand.

The barman nodded at the glass. "It looks like you needed that."

Pike nodded, picked up the glass and drained it. He handed the glass to the barman. "Pull me another."

The barman took the glass. "Sure," and pulled him another pint of Worthington's.

Pike took another long drink and put the half empty glass down on the bar. He nodded to the barman. "Thanks. I needed that."

The barman leaned forward on the bar. "Are you local?"

"Used to be. This is my first visit back in ten years."

"Visiting family?"

Pike shook his head. "No. Hoping to lay some ghosts to rest and to do some business." He picked up the half empty glass and drained it.

The barman shook his head. "Steady on mate. You should eat something before you have another."

Pike nodded. "You're right. Can I order food here?"

"Sure. I'll get you a menu."

Pike held up his hand. "No need. Well done steak with chips."

"And charge it to room twenty-one." the barman added.

Pike smiled for the first time since arriving back in his home town. "Yes. Thanks."

9:00am Thursday 7th May

Pike's phone was ringing on the bedside table. He groaned, fumbled around for it and knocked it onto the floor. "Fuck!" He grabbed for the phone, focused his eyes, pressed 'answer' on the screen and croaked, "Hello."

"It's Ken. Are you okay, Bill?"

"Who?"

"Ken Williams, your Investigations Director."

Pike groaned and rubbed his face with his free hand.

"Bill?"

Pike sat up in bed and rubbed his face again. "I'm okay, Ken. Is there a problem at the office?"

"No. The office is fine. Just phoning to see what your plan is for finding Joe Crosby."

"I'm going over to his sister's house. Hopefully she'll see me." Pike could hear muffled voices in the background. "Ken?"

"Yes. Okay Bill. Sounds like a plan" and the call went dead.

Pike groaned, tossed the phone down on the pillow, pulled back the duvet and swung his legs out of bed. He groaned as he stood up, stretched his arms up towards the ceiling, scratched his balls and walked slowly to the bathroom for a shower.

Scholes Village, South Yorkshire - 11:00am Thursday 7th May

Pike was sitting in the Audi outside of the old cottage on Scholes Lane. He was nursing a headache and a strong black coffee. He took a sip. He looked over at the cottage, it hadn't changed since he was a boy. The rose garden in the front was just starting to bloom and the ivy creeping up the stonework had been neatly cut back around the old, green front door and the windows. He sighed, massaged his temple and took another sip of coffee.

The front door of the cottage opened, and Sally Crosby stepped out into the warm sunny morning. She locked the door behind her and walked down the old stone path in front of the windows, to the small, white Toyota parked on the gravel driveway. She opened the driver's door, threw her shoulder bag onto the front passenger seat and got into the car.

Pike smiled. Sally looked good for a woman in her late fifties. Her blonde hair was immaculately styled around her ears and into the nape of her neck, the fitted, striped blouse showed off her breasts and the faded tight jeans accentuated her figure. She was still beautiful, and Pike's heart began to beat faster. He strained to see if she was wearing a wedding ring, but he was too far away to see if she was. He took another sip of coffee.

The Toyota pulled out of the driveway, turned right and drove past the parked Audi. Pike tried to melt into the soft, black, leather seats.

Sally Crosby noticed the man trying to shrink himself in the Audi's driver seat. She thought that he looked like an older version of Bill Pike. She looked in the rear-view mirror but could not see the man's face clearly. She shook her head and thought *it couldn't be Bill Pike, could it? No, it couldn't be, he hadn't been home in ten years.* She quickly dismissed the thought and concentrated on the road ahead, as it rose up the hill and to the right out of the village.

Pike threw what was left of his coffee out of the window and the cardboard cup into the front passenger footwell. He let the Toyota get about thirty meters ahead of him, before he started the engine. He put the car into drive, let off the handbrake and pulled quickly away from outside of the cottage.

The Toyota disappeared around the right-hand bend and Pike pressed down on the accelerator pedal. His tailing skills were rusty but it was all coming back to him. He smiled to himself and began to feel like he was enjoying working in the field again.

Rose Cottage, Scholes Village - 1:00pm Thursday 7th May

Pike had followed Sally Crosby around the shops at Meadowhall shopping mall and then back to her cottage. Not once had she shown any indication that she knew she was being followed and Pike was relieved that his tailing skills had returned to him very quickly. A confrontation with Sally in public would have been disastrous for finding out where Joe, her brother was. He decided to park the Audi in the car park behind the Bay Horse pub down the lane and walk up to the cottage. He tried to rehearse what he would say to Sally on the walk to the cottage, but he could not find the right words and he swore out of frustration.

Pike raised his right arm to knock on the old, green door and noticed it shaking. "Fuck," he said under his breath and grabbed his wrist with his left hand. The shaking stopped. He counted to ten, took a deep breath and knocked hard, twice.

The door opened a few seconds later. Sally Crosby stood in front of him, her face a picture of total surprise.

Pike smiled. "Hello Sal."

She did not say anything. She just stood there with one hand on the door latch and the other over her mouth.

There was an awkward minute's silence and then she stepped aside, inviting Pike into the cottage without saying a word.

Pike stepped through the doorway and into the familiar hallway, the dark oak staircase to his right, a now faded and worn dark red hallway carpet leading to the kitchen and faded flowery paper on the walls.

Sally closed the door behind him and walked down the hallway into the kitchen.

Pike followed. "You need to redecorate Sal."

Sally ignored the comment and leaned on the old, oak kitchen table. She looked Pike up and down. His greying blonde hair was neatly combed back with a parting on the left side, the dark blue suit was tailored with narrow lapels and the skinny, dark blue tie was tied with a windsor knot at the collar of a crisp, white cotton shirt. As always, his black, oxford shoes were highly polished. She studied his face, it had more lines than she remembered. His stubble was greying, and his eyes were dark and lifeless, even when he smiled. "What are you doing here?"

Pike smiled and pushed his hands into his suit trouser pockets. "It's good to see you Sal."

Sally ignored the comment. "What are you doing here, Bill?"

Pike sighed and looked down at his feet. "I need your help, Sal."

Sally just stared at him.

"I need to speak to Joe."

Anger immediately rose in Sally, but she managed to speak calmly. "Leave Joe alone you bastard. He lost everything because of you."

Pike shifted his weight from his right leg to his left. He looked Sally dead in the eye. "Sal, I wouldn't be here if it wasn't important. He's our last hope to find a man who's been missing for a long time. I need to speak to him. Even if it's a very short conversation, which ends with him telling me to fuck off."

There was a long few minute's silence as Sally studied the man before her from her past. She broke the silence. "You want a cup of tea, Bill?"

"Yes. Thanks."

Pike watched Sally as she moved around the kitchen making the pot of tea and putting biscuits out on a plate. He smiled to himself. "I remember your mother putting biscuits out on a plate for us when we were kids."

Sally stopped and looked at the plate in her hand. She let out a short laugh. "She did, didn't she."

Pike continued, "We used to sit round this table drinking pop and eating custard creams."

After a few moments of silent memories, Sally put the plate of biscuits down on the kitchen table, picked up the teapot and poured two mugs of tea. "Put your own milk and sugar in," she said flatly.

"Thanks." Pike said smiling.

She forced a smile back.

They sat at the kitchen table and drank their tea in silence. Each stole quick glances at the other and hoped that they would not be seen.

Sally put her mug down on the kitchen table. "I'm not telling you where Joe is."

Pike's mug hovered just in front of his mouth.

His eyes were pleading. "Sal, we really need Joe's help. He's our last hope of finding this missing man."

She glared at him. "Rosie got killed, Joe nearly lost his life and it was all because you were in the bottom of a bourbon bottle. Joe's in a good place now. He's happy and I don't want you back in his life."

Pike nodded and took a drink of tea. "You always looked out for him Sal, but this is important."

Sally slapped her hand down onto the kitchen table. "To who? To the firm? To you?"

Pike shook his head. "No Sal. To Lord and Lady Grant. Their son, William, has been missing a long time and they want to know if he's alive or dead."

There was a long minute's silence and it was now Sally's turn to look across the table with pleading in her eyes. She sighed, "Bill, I lost Joe for 4 years, no emails, texts or phone calls and….."

Pike cut her off. "So you'll understand the anguish that Lord and Lady Grant have been going through. No, the anguish they are going through."

Sally shook her head. "No Bill. I'm not going to lose Joe again. He's moved on and he's happy. Leave him alone. Please, let him be."

Pike sighed. He could see the hurt in Sally's eyes. He nodded, rose from his chair, buttoned his suit jacket and turned and left the kitchen. He closed the front door quietly behind him.

Sally put her head in her hands and cried uncontrollably, her tears forming a small puddle on the kitchen table.

The Chorlton Hotel, Rotherham - 7:00pm Thursday 7th May

Pike looked around the hotel dining room and shook his head at the sight. There were lots of tables with only one man sitting at them and he thought to himself, *the lonely existence of the travelling businessman.* As he picked up the glass of iced water, his phone started ringing on the table. He put the glass down and picked up the phone. He did not recognise the number. "Hello. This is Bill Pike."

"I didn't know if you still had the same number."

"Sal?"

"I've thought hard about what you said about those people needing to know what has happened to their son, so I'll tell Joe that you're here and want to talk to him."

"Thanks."

"Don't thank me. Joe will decide if he wants to speak to you and I hope that he doesn't."

There was a long minute's silence and Sally broke it. "Good night Bill."

"Sal?"

"What?"

"Have you had dinner yet?"

"No. Not yet."

"Come and join me for dinner. I'm at the hotel next to the………."

Sally cut him off "No thanks. I don't want to see you again Bill. Never again, you hear me? Never again." She ended the call.

Pike put the phone down on the table, picked up the glass of iced water and took a sip. He looked around the restaurant again at the men eating dinner alone and suddenly he was not hungry. He put the glass of water down on the table, rose from his chair and headed for the bar, thinking *at least there is a small chance that Crosby will call me.*

Sally Crosby was exhausted. She had not been to bed but had sat in the old, high backed leather chair beside the log burner all night. She had resisted the temptation to drown her emotions in a bottle of vodka and instead, she had had conversations inside her head with herself, about why she should or should not tell her brother that Bill Pike was looking for him. The matter had been more complicated by the fact that she had been reckless and had already told Pike that she would tell Joe.

She closed her eyes and massaged her temples to ease the searing headache. It did not work, the pressure inside her head was increasing. She shook her head and sighed. She picked up her phone from the chair arm and pressed one on speed dial for her brother.

The call was answered on the third ring. "Good morning Sal."

"Hello Joe. I need to see you this morning."

"Sounds serious. Is everything okay?"

Sally ignored the question. "I'll be at your place within the hour."

Joe hesitated and waited a couple of seconds for his sister to continue speaking. She did not. "Okay. See you soon."

Sally ended the call.

Crosby looked at the phone screen for a few seconds, shrugged and put it into the pocket of his old scruffy jeans.

Sally had always been a bit of drama queen and he shook his head. He went back to checking tomato plants in the big greenhouse behind the house.

Back Lane Market Garden, Rotherham - 9:45am Friday 8th May

Sally turned her car right onto the country lane and then immediately left into the market garden. She parked in front of the old stables, got out and was greeted with a hug and a smile by her brother's partner.

"Hi Sal."

"Good morning, Caitlin" and she returned the hug.

"Joe's in the kitchen making coffee. I'll leave you two to talk."

Sally put her hand on Caitlin's arm and stopped her from walking away. She shook her head. "No. You should hear this too, it's important."

Caitlin saw concern in Sally's eyes. "Errm, okay." She took hold of Sally's hand and led her into the house.

Crosby turned around from the coffee machine on the kitchen work top as Caitlin and Sally walked into the kitchen. His face lit up with a beaming smile when he saw his sister. He walked across the kitchen, gave her a bear hug, which lifted her off her feet, and kissed her on the cheek. "Coffee's made. Want one?"

Sally smiled. "Yes, please and make it Irish."

Crosby studied his sister's face for a moment and said, "It's a bit early for that, Sal."

"Joe, the stronger the better for what I've got to say."

Crosby shook his head. "Okay," and he walked back across the kitchen and poured steaming, black coffee into three, large, red mugs. He added cream and sugar into Caitlin's mug and gave Sally her mug of coffee, along with a small bottle of Irish whiskey, which he had gotten out of a cupboard above the coffee machine. He drank his coffee black.

Sally sat down at the kitchen table, poured two caps full of whiskey into the mug, picked up a tea spoon from the table and stirred. She looked her brother quickly up and down while she stirred and thought he looked like a tramp. He had long hair and a bushy beard, and was wearing an old, faded checked shirt with the sleeves rolled up above his elbows, faded jeans with rips in each knee and worn out old walking boots. She shook her head. "You look scruffier each time I see you, Joe."

Crosby grinned. "Sod off, Sal."

Sally cradled the mug of coffee in both hands and took as sip. "Mmmmm. Nice coffee."

Crosby raised his mug to his lips and blew softly into it. He took a sip. "It's a new Columbian blend." He put his mug down on the work top next to the bread maker and looked across the kitchen at his sister, who was taking another sip of coffee. "Sal, it sounded like there was something important you wanted to talk to me about. What's going on?"

Sally looked up with a grave look on her face.

"Sal, what's going on?" Caitlin asked.

Sally sighed and looked her brother dead in the eye. "Bill Pike's looking for you. He came to the cottage yesterday."

Colour instantly drained from Crosby's face. "What?"

"He wants to speak to you."

Crosby was battling to stop himself shaking. "What…. what about?"

Sally shook her head and sighed. "He wants you to help find an aristocrat's missing son. I just told him that I would tell you that he wanted to speak to you, and that it would be your decision if you wanted to talk to him."

Caitlin spoke up. "Bill Pike. Your best friend from school and old business partner?"

Crosby picked up his mug of coffee. The mug shook in his hand. He nodded, steadied the cup in both hands and took a sip.

Silence descended upon the kitchen as Crosby, Sally and Caitlin sipped their coffee.

A knot grew in Crosby's stomach and he felt sick. He put the mug down on the work top and studied the old, worn out boots on his feet.

Caitlin broke the silence. "What are you going to do Joe?"

Crosby looked across at Sally. "You didn't tell him where I live, did you?"

Sally shook her head. "No."

He looked at Caitlin, his eyes pleading *help me out here.*

Caitlin smiled back at him. "Sal, me and Joe need to talk this over."

Sally nodded. "Of course." She smiled thinly at

her brother and continued, "Bill's on the same old mobile number, if you decide to call him."

Crosby nodded.

Sally put the mug down on the kitchen table. "I need to get going anyway, I've got some errands to run." She rose from the kitchen table, walked across the kitchen and hugged her brother tight. She kissed him on the cheek.

Caitlin put her mug down on the kitchen table and smiled as Sally let go of her brother. "I'll walk out with you to your car, Sal."

Sally opened the driver side door and turned to Caitlin. "Be careful Caitlin. Don't let Bill Pike get a foothold in Joe's life. He's a selfish bastard and will use what little soul Joe has left for his own purpose and benefit."

Caitlin hugged Sally. "Thanks. We'll have a good long talk about it."

Sally nodded, got into the car and slammed the door shut.

Caitlin watched the white Toyota turn right onto the lane and then turned towards the house. Crosby stood in the doorway with his hands in his jeans pockets. She took a deep breath, put a smile on her face and started walking towards him.

7:30pm Friday 8ᵗʰ May

Caitlin put the plate of Irish stew and dumplings down in front of Crosby and lightly brushed her hand over his cheek as she walked around the table to her place at the kitchen table. She smiled at him as she sat down.

Crosby breathed in the aroma from his plate. "I love your stew and dumplings."

She was still smiling. "Just like my mammy used to make."

Crosby cut a piece of dumpling and put it into his mouth. He closed his eyes and savoured the taste. When he opened them, Caitlin had not touched her food and was staring at him.

"What are you going to do about Bill Pike, Joe."

Crosby put his knife and fork down on his plate. He shook his head and sighed. "I don't know. I really should ignore him, he's bad news, but a part of me is curious to hear what he has to say."

Caitlin smiled softly. "Joe, you're in a really good place right now. The business is doing well, everything is really good right now."

There was a long minute's silence as Crosby and Caitlin looked at each other across the table. Caitlin broke the silence. "Look, if you want to hear what he has to say, then I think we should meet him together.

That way, we'll be both be clear about what he wants."

"You think we should meet him?"

Caitlin smiled. "My mammy used to say that it was rude to ignore someone and anyway, if we don't like what he has to say, we can tell the eejit to fuck off."

Crosby started laughing.

Caitlin stabbed a piece of potato with her fork and put it into her mouth.

When Crosby stopped laughing, he grinned at Caitlin. "I'll ask Sal to set up a meeting, somewhere neutral, and we'll catch him off guard by turning up together. I don't want him here, or to meet in pub where he'll be comfortable."

Caitlin nodded. "Why ask Sal to set up the meeting?"

"Because I don't want him to have a number he can contact me on."

"Okay. We should meet him somewhere out in the open, maybe Rother Valley Country Park, tomorrow at two?"

Crosby nodded. "Perfect. I'll call Sal after dinner."

Caitlin smiled, cut a piece of dumpling and put it into her mouth.

The conversation for the rest of dinner was light and there was laughter.

Crosby was well fed, and he leaned back in his favourite chair by the fireplace.

Caitlin smiled at him from the sofa and took a drink of coffee. She put the mug down on the wooden floor. "Tell me, what's Bill Pike's like?"

Crosby thought for a moment. "He's tall and has

rugged features. He dresses in the best tailored suits from Savile Row in London, which gives him confidence and swagger. He's not smart but he's not dumb either. He relies on common sense and thinking things through."

Caitlin nodded, picked up the mug of coffee and took a sip.

Crosby continued. "He likes a drink. In his book, it's never too early in the day for a glass of bourbon. He's loud when he talks and very persuasive. He'll talk over you to get his point across. He has an answer for everything. He says what he likes and likes what he says. He's a proper old fashioned Yorkshireman."

Caitlin took another sip of coffee. "An arse then."

Crosby let out a short laugh. "More like a drunk and a right proper bastard."

Caitlin nodded grimly. "Just like my da."

Crosby didn't hear her comment about her father. It was because of Pike that Rosie was in Belfast back in 2009 and he was now back in that dirty warehouse, watching the life ebb away from her eyes. A single tear rolled down his cheek and he quickly wiped it away with the back of his hand.

Caitlin saw the tear and knew that Joe was thinking about Rosie.

9:00pm Friday 8th May

Crosby pressed two on speed dial for Sally and drummed the fingers of his free hand the chair arm.

The call was answered on the third ring. "Hello Joe."

"Call Bill and tell him I'll meet him at Rother Valley, tomorrow at two pm."

There was a long minute's silence and then Sally said, "Call him yourself."

"No."

"Why not?"

"Because I don't want him to have a number he can contact me on directly."

Sally considered this for a long few seconds and then asked, "Are you sure you want to meet him?"

"Yes."

Sally shook her head. "Okay" and she ended the call.

Sally was still shaking her head as she stared at her phone for a few seconds. She went into the call list, took a deep breath and tapped the number on the screen for Bill Pike.

The call was answered on the first ring. "Sal. It's good to hear from you."

She ignored the greeting. "Joe will meet you at

two tomorrow at Rother Valley."

Pike let out a long, silent breath of relief. "Okay. I'll be there."

Instead of ending the call, Sally paused for a moment.

"Sal?"

"What?"

"Come and have a drink with me. For old times sake?"

"That's not a good idea Bill."

"Why not?"

"Because I don't want to get involved with you again." She ended the call, tossed the phone down on the sofa beside her and drained the glass of vodka she was holding in her other hand.

Bill Pike had re-appeared in her life after ten years and had turned her emotions upside down. She was mentally exhausted. She closed her eyes and drifted off to sleep with an empty vodka bottle resting on her lap.

Rother Valley Country Park, South Yorkshire - 2:10pm Saturday 9th May

Crosby and Caitlin sat in the old, battered, Land Rover and watched Bill Pike climb out of a grey Audi. Crosby snorted and pointed out Pike, saying, "Trust him to drive a fancy car."

Caitlin watched Pike look around the car park and towards the lake. She studied him. His blonde hair was slicked back, the dark blue suit made him look tall and slim and his white shirt looked crisp against the dark cloth. His black shoes were buffed to a bright shine and the silver tie pin holding the thin, knitted, black tie in place, glinted in the afternoon sunshine. She watched him check his appearance in the shine of the car and quickly adjust the knot of his tie. She thought that his face had lines which showed he had seen a lot of life, but he was ruggedly handsome and definitely had confidence and swagger.

Caitlin made a move to get out of the Land Rover, but Crosby put his hand on her arm. He shook his head. "No. Wait. Let the man stew for ten minutes."

Pike was getting agitated. He knew from past experience that Crosby was always early for an appointment, but today he was late. He glanced at his watch for the tenth time in the last five minutes and looked around the lake shore. He kicked at a stone and it went sailing into the lake. There was no sign of Crosby and he swore under his breath.

Crosby saw from Pike's body language that he was frustrated, and he smiled to himself at the small victory. He took a deep breath, "He's stewed enough. Let's go."

Caitlin tried to smile reassuringly at Crosby and squeezed his hand, but he ignored the gesture. He was focused on the scene through the windscreen.

Pike swore under his breath again and turned to look towards the parked cars behind him. He noticed the small, pretty, brunette getting out of an old Land Rover and then saw the bearded man in the old checked shirt and ripped jeans, slam the driver's side door shut. The couple held hands and walked towards him.

Pike studied the man. He was slim, six feet tall and walked with a straight back. His hair was longer than he remembered, and his long, scruffy beard was greying. It was definitely Crosby and he smiled to himself.

When the couple got to within six feet, Pike held out his right hand for a handshake. "Joe. It's good to see you."

Crosby ignored the greeting and glared at his old friend, "Still a smooth looking bastard I see."

Caitlin squeezed his hand.

Pike pushed his hands into his suit trouser pockets and smiled at Caitlin. "Hello. I'm Bill Pike."

Caitlin did not return the smile. "Caitlin Quinn, Joe's partner."

"Irish."

"What of it?"

"Doesn't matter."

Crosby butted in. "What do you want Bill?"

Pike's smile disappeared. "Your help."

Crosby said nothing, so Pike continued. "One of Lord Grant's sons has been missing for eighteen months."

"So what?"

"He's been missing a long time, Joe, and we're no closer to finding him. We need your help."

"I'm out of the finding game, Bill."

"Hear me out, Joe."

Crosby sighed loudly. "Go on."

"You're our last hope to find this man, Joe."

Crosby was shaking his head. "No shit, Sherlock. Over twelve months down the line...."

"Eighteen months, Joe."

"And you've not found the man. You must be bloody desperate."

Caitlin cut in. "Let's walk and talk" and she nodded right towards the lakeside path.

Pike glared at Caitlin and Crosby did not like it. His tone was sharp. "Caitlin has a say in this. Fill us both in or we leave."

Pike stared into Crosby's eyes for a long few seconds. Crosby's face was deadpan and he did not blink. A smile spread across Pike's face and he nodded. "Okay."

As the three of them stepped onto the lakeside path, Pike began to fill Crosby in on the case. "William Grant, younger twin of Robert Grant, came home from his second tour of Afghanistan on Eleventh of October Twenty Thirteen. He went out on leave a week later and blew forty grand in Blades Casino on his first night. The casino's CCTV shows him leaving alone at three thirty in the morning on Nineteenth of October and he's not been seen since."

Crosby listened to Pike without interruption. "Why do you think I can find him?"

Pike stopped walking, turned and looked Crosby in the eyes. "Because you're the best Finder in the business, Joe."

"Used to be."

Pike sighed. "Just come down to the office and go through the files. If you see any holes in the investigations, follow them up. If you think we've covered everything and there's nothing more that you can do, then that's the end of the matter."

Crosby thought for a moment and ground the sole of his right boot into the dirt path. "I'll think about it," and he turned, pulling Caitlin back towards the car park.

Caitlin glanced quickly back at Pike.

Pike stood with his hands in his suit trouser pockets and watched Crosby and Caitlin walk away. He smiled as Caitlin looked back at him and let out a long, slow, breath. He was relieved that at least, Crosby had not told him to go to hell.

Crosby got into the driver's seat of the Land Rover and slammed the door shut. He fastened his seatbelt and turned on the engine.

Caitlin stared at him. "Well?"

Crosby did not look at her. He slammed the gear stick into first and said, "I'm thinking about it." He released the handbrake and drove the Land Rover a little too quickly out of the car park.

**Back Lane Market Garden, Rotherham - 6:00pm
Saturday 9th May**

Caitlin glanced over at Crosby sitting at the kitchen table, as she took the homemade pizza out of the oven. He was deep in thought and had buried himself in the business' finances since they had arrived home from the meeting with Bill Pike. She was waiting for him to tell her what he was thinking.

Crosby looked up from the paperwork as Caitlin put the pizza down onto the large wooden block, in the middle of the table. He smiled at her as he pushed the papers aside and picked up the pizza cutter. "It looks and smells delicious."

Caitlin sat down at her place at the table and smiled back. "Thanks."

Crosby divided the pizza up, took a slice and a big bite.

Caitlin leaned forward, her elbows on the table and her chin cradled in her hands. "Tell me what you're thinking, Joe."

The slice of pizza hovered close to Crosby's mouth. "I'm not thinking anything, other than how delicious this pizza is."

She scowled at him. "You know what I mean ye damn eejit."

The pizza still hovered at Crosby's mouth. "I

haven't given Bill Pike a second thought since we got home. This paperwork couldn't wait any longer, so I ....."

Caitlin cut him off. "Is that so?"

"Yes"

Caitlin nodded. "Okay then" and she took a slice of pizza and bit into it.

They watched each other as they ate, Crosby wanting to know what Caitlin was thinking and Caitlin waiting for Crosby to bring up the subject of Bill Pike's missing person case.

Crosby broke the silence. "I suppose there would be no harm in looking at the case files. Considering that...."

Caitlin cut in. "Considering what?"

Crosby put the slice of pizza he was eating down onto the wooden block. "They've been paying me my full salary for the last six years."

Caitlin's jaw dropped.

Crosby quickly continued. "I haven't touched a penny of it. It has just been sitting there in my bank account. I didn't officially leave the firm and when I did, I was going to give every penny back. I just didn't want to go anywhere near the office and never got around to leaving."

Caitlin dropped the slice of pizza down onto the wooden block. "So we didn't have to take out that two-hundred-thousand pound loan for the business?"

Crosby shook his head. "No. I just wanted to make the business successful with you and without any ties to the past."

Anger rose in Caitlin, she scraped her chair back

noisily and stood up. "YOU'RE A FUCKING EEJIT, JOE CROSBY" and she stormed out of the kitchen, slamming the door behind her.

Crosby's shoulders slumped as he listened to Caitlin's stomping footsteps going up the stairs. He banged his right fist down on the table. "FUCK!" Everything on the table jumped.

11:00pm Saturday 9ᵗʰ May

Caitlin got into bed and turned on her side to face Crosby. "I'm glad you didn't use that money for the business."

Crosby leaned on his elbow. "Are you?"

"Yes. It wouldn't feel like our business if you had. And you're right, there's no harm in you looking at the files for that missing man. If you think there's nothing more you can do, that's the end of it. Right?"

"Yes."

"Then go to London. Get it over with and then let's get on with our lives."

Crosby smiled, "I'll need a haircut and a beard trim if I'm going into the office. Got to at least look the part."

Caitlin grinned, "I'll give you them in the morning."

Crosby leaned forward and kissed her softly on the lips.

She responded, moving her left leg over his legs and climbed on top of him. She took off her vest top, leaned forward and kissed him passionately.

9:00am Sunday 10th May

Crosby opened his eyes and tried to focus. He rubbed them and squinted as bright sunlight streamed through the gap in the curtains. He closed his eyes again and concentrated on the sounds coming from the kitchen and the smell of frying bacon.

Caitlin put bacon, sausage, fried bread, fried egg, black pudding, mushrooms and beans onto two plates. She was just about to pick the tray up when she noticed Crosby's phone on the table. She nervously looked towards the kitchen doorway and listened for any sound of Crosby coming down the stairs. There was none, so she picked up the phone and scrolled through the contacts list. She stopped at Bill Pike's number. She looked towards the kitchen door again, to make sure Crosby was not coming through it and quickly wrote the number down on a scrap of paper. She put the phone back down on the table, exactly as it was and the scrap of paper into the pocket of her sweat pants. She picked up the tray and carried it upstairs to the bedroom.

Crosby was sitting up in bed and was just putting a pillow behind his head when Caitlin walked into the bedroom with the tray. "Good morning," he beamed.

"Morning, sleepy head."

Crosby pulled back the duvet and Caitlin climbed carefully into bed, placing the tray between them.

Crosby took a plate, a knife and fork from the tray, cut into a sausage and stuffed it into his mouth. He winked at Caitlin and said, "Lovely" through a mouthful of food.

Caitlin smiled back, picked up a slice of fried bread and took a bite.

Crosby put the tray of empty plates on the floor and leaned back on his pillow. He was content and he closed his eyes.

Caitlin rested her head on his shoulder and ran her fingers though the hairs on his chest. "What are your plans for today?"

Crosby turned his head slightly towards her. "There's a few things to tidy up in the barn and then I'm going to drink coffee and read the paper."

"An easy day then?"

"Yes, and you promised me a haircut and a beard trim too."

Caitlin leaned up and kissed him on the cheek. "After a bit of this though."

Crosby slid down under the duvet and Caitlin followed. She giggled as Crosby put his hand inside the waistband of her sweat pants.

11:00am Sunday 10th May

Caitlin watched Crosby disappear into the barn and pulled the scrap of paper with Pike's number on it out of her jeans pocket. She tapped the numbers on her phone screen, tapped on 'call' and hoped to get voicemail.

The call was answered on the second ring. "Hello. This is Bill Pike."

"Oh! Hello. This is Caitlin, Joe Crosby's partner."

"This is a surprise."

"I want to speak to you about Joe."

"Okay. What's on your mind?"

"Not now. Can we meet?"

A smile spread across Pike's face. "Sure. Where and when?"

"Seven thirty, tonight, in the bar at your hotel."

The smile turned into a grin. "Okay. I'm staying at the hotel next to the sixth form college."

"I know it."

"I'll see you at seven thirty then."

Caitlin looked out of the kitchen window and saw Crosby walking towards the house. She ended the call without another word and quickly put her phone and the scrap of paper into her jeans pocket.

Pike tossed his phone onto the Audi's front passenger

seat and got into the driver's seat. He slammed the door shut, turned on the engine and then the radio. He started singing along to the song. The Temptations.

> *I've got sunshine on a cloudy day*
> *When it's cold outside I've got the month of May*
> *Well I guess you'd say*
> *What can make me feel this way?*
> *My girl....*

Crosby appeared in the kitchen and Caitlin greeted him with, "Hello," and a beaming smile. He smiled back. "You look happy."

"I am. Oh! By the way, I'm going over to Sal's tonight."

Crosby sat down at the kitchen table and picked up the Sunday morning paper. He was not really paying attention to Caitlin. "Yes. Okay," he said flatly.

Caitlin let out a long silent breath. "Great. I'm off for a walk across the fields and when I get back, I'll give you a haircut."

Crosby did not look up from the paper and did not answer her.

When the house was out of sight, Caitlin pressed two on speed dial and waited for Sally Crosby to answer.

"Good morning, Caitlin."

"Hi Sal. I'm meeting with Bill Pike tonight to talk about Joe helping out on a case and I need an alibi."

Sally shook her head. "You've already told Joe that you're coming over here?"

"Yes."

"Caitlin. Don't get involved with Bill. He likes taking away what other people have got. He's selfish and he's mean."

"Sal, I just need him to promise that he'll never contact Joe again, after he's done this job for him."

Sally could not believe what she was hearing. It felt like her legs were about to give way, so she pulled out a chair and sat down at the kitchen table. "Joe's going back into the finding game?"

Caitlin shook her head. "No. he's just having a look at the files on a case they can't solve and will see if he can help, or not. That's all."

I hope that is all, Caitlin. And yes, if Joe asks I'll tell him you were here with me."

Caitlin let out a long, low breath of relief. "Thanks, Sal."

Sally ended the call. She put her phone down on the kitchen table, shook her head and poured herself a large glass of vodka. She cursed that she was drinking so early in the day and downed it in one mouthful. She sighed heavily and poured herself another large glass full. As the glass was just about to touch her lips, she screamed and threw it at the wall. The nearly empty bottle of vodka immediately followed, and she put her head in her hands. She had a bad feeling that her brother's life was about to change for the worse and she started to cry for him.

The Chorlton Hotel, Rotherham - 7:30pm Sunday 10th May

Caitlin walked into the hotel bar and the hum of the guest's conversations hit her. She quickly scanned the room and saw Pike sitting at a table tucked away in a corner, just to the right of the bar. He was nursing a half drunk pint of beer.

Pike saw her and stood up as she walked towards the table. He quickly looked her up and down. She was wearing brown, leather ankle boots, faded, skin tight jeans and a white cotton shirt which was open to her cleavage. Her shoulder length hair was neatly styled around her face. He liked what he saw and greeted her with a welcoming smile. "It's nice to see you again, Caitlin."

She ignored the greeting and sat down.

Pike was still standing. "Can I get you a drink?"

"No, thanks."

Pike sat down, smiled and waited for Caitlin to speak.

Caitlin studied Pike's face. He had large furrows in his brow and bags under his eyes. He looked tired. "I want you to promise that when Joe's finished on this case, that you'll never contact him again."

Pike leaned back in his chair. "He's going to help us out?"

"Yes. He'll phone you to confirm that he'll look at the files."

Pike grinned and nodded.

Caitlin continued. "And, he doesn't know I'm here. He's never to know, do you understand?"

Pike nodded. "Got it. I'll sound surprised and grateful when he phones."

"Make sure that you do."

Caitlin was about to get up from the table and leave, when Pike asked, "How did you and Joe meet?"

She thought for a moment, considering if she should answer. She decided that she would. "I met him the day he arrived in Tralee. I had just finished a shift at the hospital and was in the pub for a few drinks with the other nurses, before going home. Joe was sitting at a table in the corner by the fire, just staring at full pint of Guinness on the table in front of him. He looked so sad. She slightly shook her head at the memory.

"And?"

"He looked up and I caught his eye. Something inside me said *go over and talk to him*, so I did."

Pike smiled and reached for his glass. "What happened?"

"To cut a long story short, he had just arrived in town and had nowhere to stay, so I took him home with me. He cooked me a terrible breakfast in the morning."

Pike let out a short laugh. "Rosie always said Joe was a terrible cook, the only man who could burn a boiled egg, she used to say."

Crosby never talked about Rosie and what little Caitlin knew about her, was from very short conversations she had tried to have with Joe about her.

She saw an opportunity to learn more about Rosie, so she decided to quiz Pike about her. "I'll have that drink now. A gin and tonic please."

Pike raised his eyebrows and smiled. "Okay, sure," and he got up from the table and went to the bar to get the drink.

A few minutes later, Pike put the gin and tonic down on the table in front of Caitlin and a new pint of Worthington's down next to his half drunk pint. She took a sip and half smiled. "That's nice," she said to herself quietly.

Pike drained what was left of his old pint and picked up his new pint of Worthington's. He took a long drink, put the glass down and wiped his mouth with the back of his hand.

Caitlin shook her head. "You can put it away."

Pike ignored the comment.

Caitlin continued. "Tell me about Rosie and how she died."

"Joe's not told you."

She shook her head. "No. he refuses to talk about her and how she died."

Pike sighed. "Okay. Rosie was nothing like you. She was tall and skinny, had shoulder length blond hair and pale blue eyes. She could be prickly, not afraid to say what she thought. Joe liked her for that; he said that he always knew where he stood with her."

Pike picked up his drink and took a large mouthful.

Caitlin ran her forefinger around the top her glass and asked, "Why was she in Belfast?"

Pike picked up his glass and shook his head.

"That was my fault. I should have been in Belfast backing Joe up, but my wife had just left me, and I wasn't taking it well. I'd found refuge in the bottom of quite a few bourbon bottles and became a drunk. It's not something I'm proud of." He sighed and took another long drink."

Caitlin took a drink from her own glass and studied Pike's face. His eyes were full of sadness. She waited for him to continue.

Pike drained his glass and put it down onto the table. He continued the story. "Anyway, Joe had tracked down the missing girl, Maria McClure, to an old, disused, warehouse and said he needed back up to get her away from the kidnappers." He was looking at the table and shaking his head at the memory. He took a deep breath. "I was off the rails, drinking all day, sleeping where I passed out. I couldn't be found, so Rosie went to help Joe."

Pike picked up his glass, realized it was empty and put it down. He continued. "Rosie was fearless. She was a good shot and could handle herself in a fight. Anyway, the girl's rescue went sideways, there was a shootout and Rosie was killed."

Pike reached for his glass and remembered that it was empty before he picked it up. He sighed and shook his head.

Caitlin saw the sadness in Pike's eyes grow and she started to feel sorry for him.

Pike continued the story. "Joe was in hospital a long time, there were complications with his recovery. Anyway, he was discharged from hospital the night of the office Christmas party. He came straight from the hospital to the office and kicked the shit out of me.

Then he disappeared. That was the last time anyone at the office saw him."

Caitlin took a large mouthful of gin and tonic and put the glass down. She had the information she really wanted, why Rosie was in Belfast and why Joe hated Pike so much. "I want you to promise that when this case is over, that you will never contact Joe again."

Pike stared at her.

"Promise!" she snapped.

Pike nodded. "Okay, Sure. I promise."

Caitlin stood up, said "Good night Mr. Pike" and she turned and walked away from the table. Just before she opened the door to leave the bar, she looked over her shoulder and smiled.

Pike smiled back, half waved and watched her leave. He got up from the table as the door closed and went to the bar. He handed his glass to the barman. "A pint of Worthington's, please."

The barman nodded, took the glass and went to the Worthington's pump.

Pike let out a long sigh. Telling the story of Rosie's death had brought back sad and painful memories that he tried every day to keep locked away deep inside him. He needed another drink.

Rose Cottage, Scholes Village - 8:00pm Sunday 10th May

Sally Crosby poured herself a large glass of vodka and sat down in the soft, leather, high backed chair next to the fireplace. She looked across and smiled thinly at Caitlin.

Caitlin put her glass of gin and tonic down on the coffee table in front of the sofa. "I came so that you wouldn't have to lie to Joe."

Sally nodded and took a large mouthful of vodka.

Caitlin continued, "Bill Pike told me why Joe and Rosie were in Belfast."

Sally shook her head. "Don't get involved with that man, Caitlin."

Caitlin studied Sally for a long minute. "Why do you hate him so much?"

Sally took another large mouthful of vodka and looked Caitlin straight in the eye. "Because I know exactly what he's like and capable of."

"How do you know?"

Sally sighed. "I was married to the bastard for ten years."

Sally's bottom jaw dropped. "You were marred to Bill Pike?"

"Yes."

"What happened?"

"His drinking and his gambling became more important to him than our relationship. And then there were the other women, lots of other women."

Caitlin picked up her drink and drained it. "You left him just before Rosie got killed?"

Sally sighed. "Yes. A week before." She picked up the vodka bottle from the floor beside her chair and offered it to Caitlin, who shook her head.

Sally studied Caitlin's face and saw pity in her eyes. "I had left Bill only a week before Rosie was killed." A tear rolled down her cheek as she continued. "So, I guess, I'm responsible for Bill really going off the rails, for Rosie being in Belfast and all of Joe's unhappiness since then."

Caitlin held out her hand. Sal, pass me that bottle, I think I do need another drink."

Sally wiped away her tears and tried to smile. "I don't want to talk about Bill Pike any more, Caitlin. The man causes only pain to those around him."

Caitlin nodded as she filled her glass with vodka and took a large mouthful.

The two women sat in silence nursing their drinks. Sally wished that Pike had not reappeared, and Caitlin wondered whether it was after all, a good idea for Crosby to go back to his old office and look at the case of the missing man.

Back Lane Market Garden, Rotherham - 10:30pm Sunday 10th May

As Caitlin pulled the old Land Rover into the market garden courtyard, she saw the light on in the barn. She parked in front of the barn doors, got out and heard the music. She stood still and listened. Keane.

Trying to make a move just to stay in the game
I try to stay awake and remember my name
But everybody's changing and I don't feel the same…

Crosby was singing along at the top of his voice and was just finishing waxing his red, 1964 TR4.

Caitlin grinned when she saw Crosby dancing, nodding and singing along to the song as he gently rubbed the soft buffing cloth over the bonnet. She raised her voice, so she could be heard over the song, "It looks nice. It's a shame it doesn't run."

Crosby stopped mid-dance, looked up and grinned. He put the buffing cloth down on the bonnet, walked around to the driver's door, opened it and got into the car. He turned the key and gently pressed the accelerator pedal down. The car started first time and the engine purred. He smiled and nodded approvingly to himself.

Caitlin walked around the car, lightly running her fingers across its paintwork. "It's beautiful."

Crosby got out of the car and looked it over from front to back. "She's a classic. My Uncle John would be so proud to see his car looking and sounding this good." He ran his fingers lovingly over the top of the driver's door, leaned into the car and turned the engine off. He walked around the car to Caitlin, gently kissed her on the lips and asked, "Sal have much to say?"

A knot tightened in Caitlin's stomach. Oh, you know. Just girl talk and few drinks."

"Smells like more than just a few. You should have left the Land Rover at Sal's and got a taxi home."

Caitlin waved her hand to dismiss Crosby's comment and nodded at the TR4. "She really is beautiful." It was an attempt to divert Crosby's attention away from the amount of alcohol she had consumed.

A smile spread across Crosby's face as he looked back at the car.

Caitlin needed to escape the conversation about her night with Sally, so she kissed Crosby on the cheek and said that she was tired and going to bed. She left him admiring the old sports car.

Pike had only taken a mouthful of his sixth pint of Worthington's, when he decided that he needed to see Sally. He was over the legal limit for driving, but he did not care. He had just arrived outside of her cottage and turned off the Audi's lights, when he saw Caitlin leave the cottage and climb into the old Land Rover. He decided to follow her. He thought it would be useful to know where Joe Crosby lived.

Fifteen minutes later, Pike switched off the

Audi's lights and watched Caitlin go into the barn. "So, this is where you're hiding, Joe" he said to himself.

He switched on the car's lights and drove away before he was seen.

Crosby had never deleted Pike's number from his phone and he was now staring at it on the screen. He sighed, tapped the number on the screen, looked out of the bedroom window into night and waited for the call to be answered.

"Hello, this is Bill Pike."

"I'll come down to the office and look at the files."

"Joe, that's great news," Pike said sounding surprised.

"If I see something that's been missed, I'll follow it up but if I see no further lines of enquiry, I'm coming straight home and you never contact me again. Agreed?"

"Yes."

"Good. I'll be on an early morning train tomorrow. Have all the files ready and waiting for me in a private office, or I'm turning around and coming home."

"Okay."

Crosby ended the call and let out a long exhale of breath. A knot tightened in his stomach and a sudden wave of wanting to be sick swept over him.

Bill Pike punched the air with a "Yesssssss!" Caitlin had told him that Crosby would have a look at the files, but he had not wanted to believe it until he heard Crosby speak the words. He quickly sent a text to his secretary, telling her to get the files ready for Crosby first thing in the morning and then he went to bed a happy man.

Caitlin walked into the bedroom from the en-suite bathroom, just as Crosby tapped 'End Call' on the phone screen. "Are you all packed?"

Crosby looked up from his phone and admired the curvy, young woman standing in front of him, wearing short shorts and a vest top. "Yes. Packed enough clothes for two nights."

Caitlin looked at the suitcase. "Only two nights?"

Crosby nodded. "It should only take me two days to look at the files. If I have to stay longer, I'll buy new clothes."

Caitlin walked over to him, reached up, put her arms around his neck and kissed him softly on the lips. "I hope it is only two days."

Crosby kissed her back. "Me too."

"Where are you staying?"

Crosby answered without thinking. "At my house in Fulham."

Caitlin broke away from him, stepped back and crossed her arms. "What! You never told me that you had a house on London."

Crosby held his arms out, pleading. "I never got around to selling it."

Caitlin glared at him and shouted, "WHAT ELSE HAVEN'T YOU TOLD ME, JOE?"

"Caitlin. I........."

"WHAT ELSE?"

Crosby shifted his weight from his right leg to his left leg, put his hands into his jeans pockets and looked his shoes.

Caitlin put her hands on her hips. "WELL!"

Crosby looked up, opened his mouth, but no sound came out.

Caitlin shook her head. "YOU'RE A BLOODY EEJIT AND YOU CAN SLEEP IN THE SPARE ROOM TONIGHT." She stormed back into the bathroom, slamming the door behind her.

Crosby sat on the bed, shook his head and swore under his breath.

Doncaster station - 8:00am Monday 11th May

Crosby took his suit jacket off, folded it neatly and stowed it in the luggage rack above his seat. He looked up and down the first class carriage and shook his head as an army of laptops and phones began to appear at the other tables in the carriage. He pitied the businessmen and women who felt they had to work on their daily two hour morning journey to London Kings Cross, instead of relaxing and being ready for a hard day in the office.

The sound of tapping on laptop keys had begun. Crosby shook his head again, sat down in his seat and looked out of the window as the train pulled away from the platform. He sighed loudly and the man opposite him, looked up from his laptop, pushed his rimless glasses up his nose and made a 'tutting' sound.

The day had not gotten off to a good start. Caitlin had kissed him icily on the cheek as he left the house and he was in no mood to deal with the businessman opposite. Now he was on his way to his least favourite place in the world, the office. He shook his head again, sighed and waited for another 'tut'. It did not come; the businessman was engrossed in whatever was on his laptop screen.

As the end of the station platform disappeared, Crosby looked at his reflection in the window and thought to himself that in his dark navy blue suit, white shirt and dark burgundy knitted tie, he did not look any different to the army of businessmen on the train. He did not like what he saw, and his mood got blacker. Caitlin was not speaking to him, he had not worn a suit in six years and was feeling uncomfortable in it, and he was on his way to a place he thought he would never see again. Sadness quickly washed over him and a tear rolled down his cheek. He quickly wiped it away with the back of his hand, before the man opposite him noticed that he was upset.

Brightside Insurance, Chancery Lane, London - 11:00am Monday 11th May

Crosby paused, took a deep breath and pushed open one of the glass double doors to the office reception area. He stepped into the plush reception area, pulling his suitcase behind him and was greeted by a smiling receptionist. "Good morning. How can we help you today?"

Crosby looked around the reception area. It looked exactly as he remembered, neutral colours, art on the walls, large plants in the corners, modern lights and a thick, dark red carpet underfoot.

The receptionist was still smiling. "Sir?"

Crosby took his attention away from the cityscape painting on the wall behind the receptionist and forced a smile back. He studied the young woman for a moment, perfectly styled shoulder length blonde hair, only a little makeup, floral summer dress with a plunging neckline, long slender fingers with perfectly manicured fingernails and no engagement or wedding ring. "What's your name love?"

The receptionist hesitated for a moment and her smile disappeared. "It's Scarlet."

Crosby was still forcing his smile. "How long have you worked here, Scarlet?"

The receptionist stood up. "Look, sir. If there's.."

Crosby interrupted her with a wave of his hand. "Please. Indulge me."

"One year in July."

Crosby nodded. "It's nice to meet you Scarlet. Could you please let Ken Williams know that Joe Crosby has arrived and don't worry love, I know the way to his office."

As the receptionist dialed the fat Investigations Director's telephone extension, and before she could stop him, Crosby was on his way through the opaque glass doors to her right, leading into the main office. She panicked. "Sir.....Oh! Mr. Williams.....Fuck!"

Crosby was gone, and the door had swung closed behind him.

Bill Pike's secretary, Kelly Mathers, looked up from her laptop screen and thought she was seeing a ghost standing at the far end of the office. He was looking around, taking in the scene. The man was thinner than when she last saw him, he now had a neatly trimmed, greying beard and his hair was longer than she remembered. He looked tall and handsome in the dark navy blue tailored suit, but it was the trademark dark burgundy oxford shoes that really gave him away. It was definitely Joe Crosby and her smile spread into a grin across her face. She stood up, stepped from behind her desk and walked quickly down the office. When she was only a couple of paces away, she said loudly, "It's so good to see you, Joe."

The office stopped work and stared.

Crosby looked around the office and as he turned back to the secretary, a genuine smile spread across his face and he said, "Hello Red."

The secretary threw her arms around Crosby's neck and planted a kiss on his cheek. She then stepped back so she was at arm's length and quickly looked him up and down. Words tumbled out of her mouth. "It's been years since I was called 'Red.' I can't believe you're here. It's been a long time. I've missed you. Welcome back."

Crosby was feeling uncomfortable at being the centre of attention and held up a hand to try and curb the secretary's enthusiasm. He looked around the office at the familiar and unfamiliar faces staring at him.

Seeing that Crosby looked uncomfortable, the secretary turned to the office. "Back to work everybody, there's nothing to see here." She then linked her arm through Crosby's. "C'mon, I'll take you to your office. The files you need are out on the conference table waiting for you."

After a few steps, the secretary stopped, turned to Crosby and grinned. "It's so good to have you back, Joe."

Crosby shook his head. "Kelly, I'm not back. I'm just helping out on this one case. Then I'm gone for good."

The secretary was still grinning. "We'll see, Joe. We'll see."

Kelly opened the office door and stepped aside as Crosby stepped into the office. She followed him in and waved her right hand around the office. "There's the files on the conference table, laptop is on the desk and I'm your secretary while you're here. If you need anything just shout like you used to do. It'll be just like the old days, master and servant."

Crosby did not hear the last comment as he looked around the office, it was bare and soulless. He sighed loudly.

"It's a spare office we have at the moment, Joe."

Crosby nodded and stepped towards the desk.

The secretary started to close the door.

"Leave it open, Kelly." Crosby said without turning around.

The secretary watched Crosby for a few minutes and then returned to her desk still grinning. She was thrilled to have her old boss back.

Crosby sat down behind the desk and opened the laptop. He looked at the screen and then over at the files on the conference table. He sighed, and his shoulders slumped. He never thought that he would be back in the office again and the thought depressed him.

11:15am Monday 11th May

The young investigator walked over to Kelly's desk and smiled. "Who's that in the spare office, Kelly?"

The secretary looked up from her laptop. "None of your business Lee."

The investigator did not move. He wanted an answer.

Anger flashed in the secretary's eyes. "Look! It's Joe Crosby. Okay!" the secretary snapped.

The investigator pushed his hands into his suit trouser pockets and looked towards the open office door. "Thanks. I'll go and introduce myself," and he started walking towards the open office door.

The secretary shook her head and watched the young investigator walk towards Crosby's office. She shouted after him. "I WOULDN'T ADVISE IT, LEE."

He ignored her.

Crosby looked up as the young investigator stepped into his office. He took five steps towards the conference table with his right hand stretched out for a handshake. "I'm Lee Jones. Good to meet you Mr. Crosby."

Crosby pushed his glasses up his nose and leaned back in his chair. He quickly looked the young man over from head to toe and decided that he did not like him. "Fuck off."

The investigator hesitated, unsure of how to respond, his outstretched arm hovering in mid-air over the conference table. He decided to try again. "Mr. Crosby, I'm...."

Crosby clasped his hands behind his head. "Do you not understand English lad? Or do you have a hearing problem? I'm busy, so fuck off and go and bother someone else."

The young investigator's shoulders slumped, and he withdrew his hand. He turned and walked out of the office without saying another word. Crosby did not see him leave, his nose was already back in the file he was reading before he was interrupted.

Kelly Mathers grinned as the young investigator walked quickly out of Crosby's office and back to his desk. "I DID WARN YOU," she shouted after him.

He shot her an icy look as he slumped down in his chair in the huff.

Opposite him, the bald investigator's furious pen clicking stopped as he looked over the top of his laptop. "I see you've met Joe Crosby then."

The young investigator ignored the comment and continued his sulking.

The bald investigator let out a short laugh and the pen clicking started again.

1:00pm Monday 11th May

Kelly stepped into the doorway of Crosby's office and smiled at the sight. Crosby had loosened his tie and undone the top button of his shirt and rolled up his shirt sleeves. Both elbows were on the table with his chin resting in both hands and his glasses had slipped down his nose as he read the file. It was a sight she had seen a thousand times before and she suddenly realised that it was a sight she missed seeing.

Crosby felt a presence in the room, looked up and moved his glasses to on top of his head.

"I've brought you lunch, Joe."

Crosby waved the secretary in and she sat down at the table next to him. She pushed a pre-packaged chicken salad sandwich, a bag of ready salted crisps and a bottle of water towards him.

Crosby picked up the sandwich box. "Thanks."

Kelly sensed a question coming. "What?"

Crosby put the half opened sandwich box down onto the table. "I never expected a fanfare, but none of the old faces have been by to say hello. Why are you being so nice?"

The secretary grinned. "That's an easy one, Joe. It's Monday and you're a grumpy bugger."

Crosby stared blankly at her.

"Look, I was your secretary for years and I've

always liked you. Nothing has changed as far as I'm concerned. Now, eat your sandwich and be glad of the company."

Crosby grinned and tore open the sandwich packaging.

Through a mouth full of bread, chicken and salad, Crosby asked, "Who was that young lad who came to see me?"

Kelly grunted. "Lee Jones. He's a slimy toad but management see him as a rising star."

Crosby put his sandwich down on the table. "Really?"

"Yes."

"Well, lucky for him that I'm not back."

Kelly grinned. "We'll see if you're back or not, Joe. We'll see" and she took a bite out of her ham salad sandwich.

5:30pm Monday 11th May

Crosby had been staring at a photograph of William and Robert Grant for an hour and had been scribbling down notes. Both men had shaved heads and hazel coloured eyes, the same long thin nose and thin lips. But there was something in the photograph that bothered him, and he could not put his finger on what it was. He slammed his pen down onto the conference table in frustration and shouted, "KELLY! COME IN HERE, PLEASE."

The secretary appeared in the office doorway and Crosby waved her in, his eyes still on the photograph.

"I was just about to go home, Joe."

Crosby continued to wave her into the office. "Come and have a look at this photo and tell me what you see."

Kelly sighed quietly, walked around the conference table and sat down beside Crosby, who slid the photograph in front of her, saying, "William Grant is on the left and Robert Grant is on the right. I've written down on the pad what I see." He pushed the pad towards her and continued, "If you didn't know who was who, how can you tell them apart?"

Kelly studied the photograph for a few seconds. "The freckles over their eyebrows."

Crosby picked up the photograph and looked at it for a long few seconds. He turned and smiled at the secretary. "Clever girl. Thanks."

Kelly stood up from the table and Crosby put the photograph down. "What are you doing now?"

Kelly looked down at Crosby and shrugged. "I told you, I'm going home."

"Did you?"

"Yes."

"When?"

Kelly shook her head. "It doesn't matter."

"Have you got plans for tonight?"

"Why are you asking?"

"Have you?"

Kelly sighed "No. And I've no husband, boyfriend or pets to go home to either," she said with a hint of irritation in her voice.

Crosby leaned back in his chair. "Good. I need your help. I need a second pair of eyes to go through the files, to see if anyone has mentioned those freckles," and he waved his hand over the files spread out over the conference table.

Kelly looked down at the files.

Crosby continued, "I have a hunch."

Kelly sat down and turned to Crosby. "But Joe, I'm just a secretary."

Crosby smiled. "In my experience, secretaries are very astute, they hear and see everything. They know what's going on in an office long before the rest of us. You saw the freckles and I didn't. You're perfect for the job."

Kelly looked at the files again and nodded. "Mr. Pike won't be back in the office for a couple of days and my work's up to date, so……. Okay, Joe, I'll help you. At least it will be something different to do."

Crosby leaned forward and pointed to three files fanned out to his left. "Great. Dive into those files there and see if there's anything in them about freckles."

Kelly reached for the top file and Crosby opened the file immediately in front of him.

Kelly was nervous. "I'm looking for any mention of freckles?"

Crosby nodded but did not look at her. "Yes, and if they are mentioned, write down the file number, the page number, the paragraph number and the line number." He pushed a yellow notepad and a pen towards her.

Kelly nodded. "Okay," and she started to read the first page in the file.

Back Lane Market Garden, Rotherham – 8:00pm Monday 11th May

Bill Pike took a deep breath, knocked on the green front door and waited.

Caitlin looked at the time on her phone, put her book, pages side down on the sofa, and got up to answer the door.

The door opened, and Pike stepped forward. He grabbed Caitlin's arms, pulled her close and kissed her passionately on the lips. She struggled for a few seconds and then responded, her tongue searching for his.

Pike pushed Caitlin backwards into the house and kicked the door closed behind him.

Caitlin pushed herself away from him and headed for the stairs.

Pike grinned and followed her.

Kelly took a drink of lukewarm coffee and looked at Crosby, who felt her eyes on him. He did not look up from the last page of the file he was reading. "What is it, Kelly?"

"You know I can be a nosey bitch, right?"

"Yes."

"Where did you disappear to?"

Crosby did not answer but continued reading. When he had finished, he closed the file and looked Kelly in the eye. His face was deadpan as he said, "Yes, you are a nosey bitch."

Kelly stared at him, waiting for an answer.

He sighed. "I needed to get far away from London, so I got on a bus and headed north to Northumberland. I spent a bit of time there and then got on a plane to Lerwick in the Shetland Islands."

"You've lived there ever since?"

Crosby shook his head. "No. I shacked up with a primary school teacher there for about a year. She was a lovely young lass with red hair, green eyes and always smiling, laughing and singing." Crosby smiled at the memory.

"What happened, Joe?"

She wanted to get married and have babies and I

didn't, so she threw me out."

"Where did you go?"

"I stayed the night in a guest house and flew to Dublin, via Edinburgh, the next day. I stayed there for a few months and then drifted around Ireland, eventually ending up in Tralee, County Kerry. That's where I met Caitlin."

Kelly nodded at Crosby's left hand. "You don't have a ring on your finger."

"We're not married."

The questions kept on coming. "Do you want to be?"

"What?"

"Married."

Crosby shook his head. "No."

"Does Caitlin know that?"

"We've never discussed marriage, so I've never told her."

"Do you have any kids?"

"No."

"Do you want kids?"

Crosby was irritated by the onslaught of questions and he sighed loudly. "Look, Kelly, I don't want kids and I don't want to be here. Okay? I'm not back."

There was a long minute's silence which Kelly broke. She was undeterred by Crosby's show of irritation. "Do you live in Ireland?"

Crosby sighed and shook his head. "No, in Rotherham, South Yorkshire, where I grew up. We grow fruit and vegetables in greenhouses and sell what we grow at local farmer's markets."

Kelly took another mouthful of lukewarm coffee. Are you happy?"

"Yes. Growing fruit and vegetables is a lot less stressful than wading through this load of crap" and he waved his hand over the files on the table. "And definitely less stressful than answering your questions. Tomato plants don't ask questions. Did you know that?"

Kelly's eyes narrowed. "I might only be a secretary, but I'm not that dumb, Joe."

Silence descended on the office again and after a couple of minutes of staring at his fingernails, Crosby turned to Kelly and had tears in his eyes. "I keep expecting Rosie to walk through that door. But I know she never will. I miss her so much, Kelly."

Kelly put her arms around Crosby's neck and pulled him close. She whispered in his ear, "We all loved her and miss her."

Crosby began sobbing and Kelly ran her hand through his hair and kissed him on the cheek.

7:00am Tuesday 12th May

Crosby and Kelly had worked through the night. Crosby closed the last file and pushed it away from him. He rubbed his eyes and yawned. He turned to Kelly. "That's good work, what do we need to follow up on?"

Kelly picked up a yellow notepad and read out the list, "How to tell the brothers apart, how well William knew his brother's wife before she married and re-visit Robert Grant and Lord and Lady Grant."

Crosby nodded. "Good. We'll listen to the tapes of the original interviews this afternoon."

Kelly yawned. "Okay."

Crosby rubbed his face. "We're both tired. Go home Kelly and get some sleep. We'll start again at three this afternoon."

Kelly yawned again and stretched her arms towards the ceiling. "Okay. At three" she confirmed. She got up from the conference table and left the office.

Crosby got up from the conference table and walked over to the soft, leather, high backed swivel chair behind his desk. He sat down and immediately felt comfortable. He leaned back in the chair and clasped his hands behind his head. He closed his eyes and drifted off to sleep.

Back Lane Market Garden, Rotherham – 7:30am Tuesday 12th May

Bill Pike crept quietly down the stairs and at the bottom he slipped on his shoes. He did not bother to tie the laces. He opened the front door and stepped out into the warm morning sunshine. He closed the door quietly behind him and walked quickly over to the Audi, parked in front of the barn. He clicked the key fob to unlock the car, opened the driver's door and flopped into the soft leather seat. He was tired, but he stifled a yawn. He pulled the driver's door closed, fastened the seatbelt, started the car and its engine purred. He put the car into 'drive,' released the handbrake and drove it slowly out of the courtyard and onto the country lane.

Caitlin turned over in bed but did not open her eyes. She did not hear the Audi leave the courtyard.

Brightside Insurance, Chancery Lane, London - 1:00pm Tuesday 12th May

Crosby was grateful that the office had a shower for those employees who cycled and ran to work. He turned on the taps and quickly stripped down to his boxer shorts. He felt the water running out of the oversized shower head, turned the heat up a notch more, dropped his boxer shorts to the floor and stepped into the cubical and under the hot water. He closed his eyes and let the warmth seep into his bones.

Thirty minutes later, Crosby fastened the last button on his shirt, checked his hair and beard in the mirror and unlocked the shower room door. He opened it and with his suitcase beside him, his towel and wash bag under his arm, he stepped out of the shower room and looked down the office at the doors leading to the reception area. They were closed. He stared at them for a long few moments, waiting for them to open, but they stayed closed. He then scanned the office; it was a buzz of quiet telephone conversations, the tapping of laptop keys and the lone, furious clicking of a pen.

He turned and started walking down the office, leaving the shower room door open. As he dragged his suitcase behind him, he saw Kelly emerge through the doors from the reception area. He stopped and studied her. She had short, perfectly styled red hair and wore only minimal make-up. She was dressed in a dark navy trouser suit, the fitted jacket showing off her curves, a white blouse open at her neck, a simple gold chain around her neck and dark navy, 2 inch heels. She walked confidently with her chin up, her shoulders back and with a straight back. She looked like a city business woman and not at all like a secretary in an investigation firm. Crosby smiled and started walking towards her.

Kelly met Crosby at his office door. She nodded at the suitcase. "Did you sleep here?"

"Fell asleep in the chair at the desk. It's a good job the office has a shower."

Kelly smiled. "It's nice, isn't it? I've used it a couple of times before I've gone out with friends straight after work."

Crosby nodded. "Get the coffees in and since you're in early, we'll make a start on the tapes."

Kelly smiled and nodded. "Okay boss," and she turned and started walking towards the kitchen.

Crosby watched her for a few seconds and then stepped into his office.

5:00pm Tuesday 12th May

Crosby pressed the stop button on the tape player and leaned back in his chair. "Was that the last tape?"

Kelly ejected the tape and put it in the holder with the other tapes. "Yes." She nodded at the tapes. "You know, we really must update to video recording. Everyone these days has a smart phone which they can record interviews on and then download onto the computer system."

Crosby stretched and yawned. "Good idea. Suggest it to Ken Williams." He yawned again and continued, "There was nothing on the tapes about the freckles or how to tell William and Robert apart."

Kelly shook her head.

Crosby sighed. "Then I guess there's more work to do on this case."

"If you say so, Joe" and the office descended into silence.

Crosby closed his eyes and drifted off to sleep.

Kelly woke Crosby up after watching him sleep for couple of minutes. "Where are you sleeping tonight?"

He woke with a start "Sorry, I drifted off for a minute there." He rubbed his face. "You asked me something. What was it?"

"Where are you sleeping tonight?"

"Why do you ask?"

"You're not sleeping in the office again tonight. I have a sofa bed you can use."

Crosby smiled. "Thanks for the offer, but I still have my house in Fulham."

Kelly smiled back. "Oh. Okay." She stood up. "Are we done for the day?"

Crosby was still smiling. "Yes. Thanks for your help."

"You're welcome," and Kelly started walking towards the office door.

Crosby closed his eyes and when he opened them a couple of seconds later, Kelly was gone.

No. 2 Cloncurry Street, Fulham, London - 6:30pm Tuesday 12th May

Crosby turned the key in the lock of the flaking, black front door and pushed the door open. He stepped through the doorway and quickly scanned the hallway and stairs. Rosie's old wax jacket hung on the end of the banister right in front of him. A wave of emotion rose up through him from his feet and he put his hand out against the wall to stop his knees from buckling underneath him. He shook his head and decided to stay the night in a hotel. He stepped backwards out of the doorway and pulled the door shut. He put the key into his suit trouser pocket, picked up his suitcase and walked down the steps to the street. He turned left and headed away from the river towards Fulham Palace Road, where he hoped to flag down a taxi to take him to the Copthorn Tara Hotel, Kensington.

Crosby went into the kitchen to make his third coffee of the day and found Kelly leaning against the worktop, waiting for the kettle to boil. She yawned and suddenly stood up straight when she noticed Crosby standing, smiling at her.

Crosby put his hands in his suit trouser pockets and his smile spread into a grin. "You get much sleep?"

"No."

"Why not?"

"I couldn't get my mind off this case."

Crosby nodded. "So, what do you think the next move is?"

Kelly rested her lower back against the worktop edge and crossed her arms. "You're testing me?"

"Yes."

"Why?"

"Answer the question."

She thought for a moment. "The tapes tell us nothing we didn't already know."

"Good. And?"

"We should ask Lord and Lady Grant how they recognised which son was which."

Crosby nodded. "Good. Make the call and set up the appointment for us to see them this morning."

Kelly stared at Crosby. "Us?"

Crosby was grinning. "Yes, us. You're part of this case now and I need a partner to work it with."

"But Mr. Pike....."

Crosby cut in, "Fuck Bill. He wanted my help on this case and I need a second pair of eyes and ears. I need someone I can trust, and I trust you."

Kelly was not sure how much help she would be to Crosby out in the field, after all, she had only ever worked as a secretary. She nervously bit her bottom lip and said, "Okay."

Crosby was still grinning, "Look, finding missing people is a game. Just think of it as a game of hide and seek. People hide, we follow the evidence and find them." He nodded towards the kettle. "The kettle's boiled," and he put his cup down on the worktop. "Coffee, strong and black please," and he turned and walked out of the kitchen.

Kelly shook her head, let out a short laugh and muttered to herself, "Hide and seek eh! Never thought of it like that," and she reached for the kettle.

Eaton Place, Belgravia, London - 11:30am Wednesday 13th May

Crosby and Kelly were shown into the morning room by the butler and were told that Lord and Lady Grant would join them shortly. They had barely taken their seats when the peer, followed by his wife, entered the room.

Crosby and Kelly stood up, shook hands and introduced themselves. Lady Grant did not speak; she just smiled through the introductions.

Lord and Lady Grant sat down together on an old, ornate, threadbare sofa. The peer's right hand gently rested on his wife's knee and Lady Grant's left hand rested on top of it.

Kelly was sat on a hard, straight backed chair and felt very uncomfortable. She was trying not to fidget too much in her seat. Her instructions were to carefully watch Lord and Lady Grant's body language and their facial expressions. She studied them closely, Lady Grant looked elegant in her tweed skirt, cashmere sweater, pearl necklace and matching earrings. Lord Grant, she thought, looked dapper in his herringbone suite, red waistcoat and bowtie. She smiled politely at them.

Crosby was comfortable on an old, soft leather chair. He looked quickly around the room and thought that it was just cluttered with old junk. He liked modern, not antique or just plain old. He smiled at Lord and Lady Grant. "Thank you for taking the time out of your day, and at such short notice to see us."

Lord Grant nodded. "Of course, you're welcome. But we are rather busy, so if we could press on."

Crosby nodded. "How did you and Lady Grant tell William and Robert apart?"

Lady Grant answered. "That is a very easy question to answer Mr. Crosby. They have small freckles above their eyebrows. William's is above his right eyebrow and Robert's is above his left."

Crosby nodded. "Was that the only way you could identify them?"

Lady Grant nodded. "Yes."

Crosby nodded again. "Did William and Robert ever switch identities?"

Lord Grant let out a short laugh. "Dear god, yes. All of the time when they were children. Created havoc at school."

Crosby shifted forward in his seat. "And as adults?"

The peer nodded. "Yes. To cause trouble just for the sake of it and of course, to get what they wanted."

Crosby thought for a moment. "What was William's relationship like with Robert's wife, before she married Robert?"

Lord and Lady Grant quickly glanced at each other.

Kelly saw Lady Grant squeeze her husband's hand and noticed their body language change from relaxed to tense.

Crosby waited patiently for an answer, knowing that people find silences uncomfortable and feel the need to fill the silence with conversation.

Lady Grant broke the silence. "Anna and William were inseparable when they were children. They even went to the same college at Oxford. We expected them to marry and it was quite a shock when Robert announced that he and Anna were engaged."

Crosby nodded and pressed on with his questions. "How did William feel about the engagement and marriage?"

Lady Grant squeezed her husband's hand again and Kelly saw it.

Lord Grant answered. "He behaved admirably. Nothing changed between him and Robert."

Crosby smiled. "William joined the army shortly after the announcement?"

Lord Grant nodded. "Yes. He went to Sandhurst and graduated top of his class," he said proudly.

Crosby thought for a moment and stood up. He held out his right hand for a handshake and thanked Lord and Lady Grant for their time.

Lady Grant's hand lingered in Crosby's. "You will find William, won't you?"

Crosby smiled. "I'm trying my very best to find him."

As Kelly walked beside Crosby down the steps of the town house, she said, "They didn't like it when you asked about William's relationship with Anna before she married his brother. And I don't believe that William reacted that well to the news of the engagement. I think he joined the army because he was hurt and so he didn't have to see Robert and Anna together."

Crosby grinned. "Good. So, what's our next move?"

Without hesitation Kelly answered "We pay Robert and Anna a visit up in Northumberland. Wherever that is."

Crosby nodded. "A trip north it is." He put his hand gently on Kelly's shoulder as they walked. "Don't worry about Bill. I'll sort him out if he spits his dummy out. And by the way, you're doing great."

A smile spread across Kelly's face.

Brightside Investigations, Chancery Lane - 1:00pm Wednesday 13th May

Kelly picked up her desk phone on the second ring. "Hello. Brightside Investigations, Kelly Mathers speaking."

"It's Bill. I'll be in the office in thirty minutes."

The call then went dead. Kelly stared at the handset for a couple of seconds, and then put it back in its place. She took a deep breath, rose from her chair and went to tell Crosby of Pike's imminent arrival.

Crosby looked up from the text he was sending when Kelly walked into his office. She looked pale. "What's wrong?"

"Mr. Pike's on his way to the office."

Crosby tapped 'send' on the phone screen. "Okay. Thanks. I'm going to make myself scarce."

Kelly nodded. "Okay" and left the office.

Crosby sank back into his chair and let out a long exhale of breath.

1:30pm Wednesday 13th May

Kelly looked anxiously down the office at the doors to the reception area, expecting to see Bill Pike appear through them at any moment. He did not, and she began typing furiously on her laptop keyboard.

The young investigator saw Kelly's frequent glances down the office and decided to find out what was going on. He walked over to her desk and startled her when he said, "Hi Kelly. You look nice today."

Kelly quickly regained her composure and rolled her eyes. "What do you want, Lee?"

The young investigator looked down the office. "Who are you expecting to come through those doors?"

Kelly's face was deadpan. "It's none of your business Lee, go and do some work."

"Seriously, Kelly, what's going on?"

A gruff South Yorkshire accent answered. "That's none of your business lad, so piss off."

Neither Kelly or the young investigator saw Crosby arrive at the desk and both were startled.

The young investigator quickly composed himself and decided to try and introduce himself again. He offered his right hand for a handshake. "I'm Lee Jones and it's……"

Crosby ignored the offered hand and glared straight into the young investigator's eyes. "I don't care who you are. Now, fuck off and get on with your work, before I have your bollocks for lunch."

Kelly put her hand over her mouth to stifle a laugh.

The young investigator withdrew his hand and went back to his desk defeated.

Kelly looked up at Crosby. "I thought you'd left."

Crosby shook his head. I had some calls to make. I'm going now. Oh! And Kelly….."

"What?"

"I know you're a woman, but seriously, you need to grow a pair if you're going to get on in this game."

Anger immediately rose in Kelly. She stood and slapped Crosby across the face. "Don't ever talk to me like that again and is that a big enough pair for you?"

The office stopped and stared.

Crosby's cheek was stinging, and as he gently rubbed it, he thought to himself *Good girl*.

Kelly was shocked at what she had just done and put her hand over her mouth. She sat down.

Crosby grinned. "You're going to do just fine."

"I'm so sorry, Joe."

"Don't be. Now, I want you to book yourself a first class train ticket to Alnmouth for tomorrow morning."

"For me? First Class?"

"Yes."

"Okay. Accommodation?"

Crosby shook his head. "No. Taken care of. I've booked two rooms in a nice little pub I know called the Fisherman's Rest. We'll be well looked after there and very comfortable. Ask for the landlady, Maggie, when you arrive. Make yourself comfortable and I'll join you tomorrow night.

Kelly nodded.

"Good. I'm off home to sort some stuff out" and Crosby turned and began walking down the office towards the glass double doors, pulling his suitcase behind him.

Kelly watched Crosby disappear through the doors and then typed *National Rail Enquiries* into the search engine on her laptop.

2:30pm Wednesday 13th May

Crosby's phone buzzed on the table, drawing his attention away from the passing farm fields. He picked it up, looked at the screen, sighed and tapped 'Answer' on the screen. "What do you want Bill?"

"Less of the animosity for starters, Joe."

Crosby ignored the comment and waited for Pike to speak.

"Joe, I hear that Kelly Mathers has been working with you on the Grant case."

"Yes. So what!"

"She's a secretary, Joe, not an investigator. If you want a second pair of eyes and ears, Lee Jones is quite capable. Could be as good as you one day."

Crosby moved his phone away from his ear and swore under his breath. After a moment's thought, he said in a matter of fact tone, "Listen Bill. Kelly's on this job with me and I expect to see her in Alnmouth tomorrow night, or I walk away, and you're fucked on this case. Got it! Good!" He ended the call and slammed his phone down on the table.

The lady sat opposite him looked up from her home and lifestyle magazine.

Crosby smiled. "Sorry."

She grinned. "It's fine. I deal with dicks all the time," and she went back to reading about curtains and blinds.

Pike looked at his phone and grinned. That was the reaction he had wanted from Crosby. He had found a partner he liked working with and if he found William Grant and felt good from the buzz of finding him, then there was a chance he would come back to the firm. In Pike's opinion, the firm had suffered in Crosby's absence and needed him back.

He got up from behind his desk and walked to his office door. "Kelly, come in here please."

Kelly immediately began to worry that she was in trouble for helping Crosby. She took a deep breath, rose from her chair and walked into Pike's office. She closed the door behind her and expected to be shouted at.

Pike stood with his hands in his suit trouser pockets and his face was deadpan. "You're promoted to Junior Investigator and will continue to work on the Grant case with Joe. You can move to the spare desk next to Lee Jones."

A smile spread across Kelly's face. "Thank you, Mr. Pike."

Pike nodded. "And find me a new secretary to start at eight am tomorrow morning."

Kelly was still grinning. "Thank you again, Mr. Pike." She turned and started to leave the office.

Pike called after her. "And Kelly, she better be as good as you."

Kelly stopped and turned. "Yes, Mr. Pike."

2:35pm Wednesday 13th May

Kelly dug her mobile phone out of her bag and pressed two on speed dial.

The call was answered on the second ring. "Hi Kelly."

"Hi Joss. Are you still looking for a job?"

"I'm on my way to an interview at Landau Robson Investigations as we speak."

"Stop. Don't go. I've just been promoted to Junior Investigator and you can have my job. No interview, twenty grand basic salary and start tomorrow at eight am. What do you say?"

There was a long pause and background street noise on the other end of the call. "Joss?"

"I'm on my way. I'll be there in twenty minutes" and the call ended.

Kelly smiled to herself and dropped her phone back into her bag. She looked over at the spare desk beside Lee Jones, who was staring intently at his laptop screen.

Opposite him, the furious pen clicker, and it suddenly irritated her.

The thought of sitting so close to them began to depress her. Her shoulders slumped, she sighed loudly and began to clear out her desk.

3:00pm Wednesday 13th May

Joss Baldwin was escorted by Scarlet, the receptionist, through the office. She waved when she saw Kelly stand up behind her new desk.

Kelly smiled and waved back. Her friend was wearing a fitted, dark grey trouser suit, a light blue blouse and three inch, dark grey heels. A small black leather bag was slung over her right shoulder. She walked with a purpose, as if she was owning the catwalk, and her blonde, shoulder length curly hair bounced as she walked. Joss was the most confident woman that Kelly had ever met.

The young investigator looked up from his laptop. "Who's your friend, Kelly?"

"None of your business, Lee" and Kelly walked around the back of the young investigator's chair towards her friend.

The two women hugged and kissed each other on the cheek.

Joss quickly scanned the office. "Who's the young guy staring at us?"

Kelly answered without turning around. "The office weasel."

Joss let out a short laugh. "He's giving weasels a bad rep."

Kelly grinned.

Joss turned her attention away from the young investigator. "So, what's your boss like, Kelly?"

Kelly glanced towards Pike's office and kept her voice low. "He's a chauvinist pig. He'll call you every inappropriate name you don't want to hear, love, dear, sweetheart and he'll try and get into your knickers."

Joss threw her head back and let out a short laugh. "You remember that senior partner I told you about, from when I worked at Killick and Co?"

"Yes."

"Well, he tried it on every day for the three years I worked for him. You should have seen the look on his face when I handed him my resignation and told him that I was a lesbian. He was devastated."

Kelly laughed and when she stopped, Joss continued. "If I can handle him, Kelly, then I can handle this guy. What's his name?"

"Bill Pike."

"Pike, that's a grumpy fish that bites, isn't it?"

"Yes. Mr. Pike certainly is grumpy and mean."

Joss noticed the drinks cabinet in Pike's office. "What does he like to drink?"

"Bourbon on the rocks. I'll introduce you."

Joss put her right hand on Kelly's left shoulder. Her pale blue eyes twinkled with mischief. "No. I'll introduce myself." She unfastened a button on her blouse to show her cleavage and walked confidently into Pike's office.

Bill Pike looked up from his laptop as the strange woman walked over to his drinks cabinet and started to put ice into one of the Stuart crystal glasses. He leaned back in his chair and clasped his hands behind his head as he took in the sight of the tall, slim, woman wearing a trouser suit, which accentuated her athletic figure. A grin spread across his face. Joss poured a double measure of bourbon over the ice, picked up the glass, turned and walked confidently over to Pike's desk. She smiled as she bent over and put the drink down on the leather writing mat in front of him.

Pike's grin grew wider as he got a good look at Joss's cleavage. "And who are you?"

Joss straightened up and was still smiling. "I'm Joss, your new secretary," and she turned and walked towards the office door.

Pike was still grinning. He picked up the drink and took a large mouthful. The liquor burned the back of his throat and just loud enough he said, "Nice."

Joss heard the comment and stopped by door. She looked over her left shoulder, winked and walked out of the office.

Kelly watched her friend and shook her head in disbelief at what she had just witnessed. When Joss was three paces away from her she said, "You're a prick tease."

Her friend grinned. "I know I am and I'm very good at it. It's fun bringing them to their knees."

Kelly rolled her eyes and shook her head again.

Joss turned and nodded towards the desk outside of Pike's office. "My desk?"

"Yes. Monday to Friday, start at eight, one hour for lunch and finish at five thirty, or when Mr. Pike says, if the firm is working on a big case."

Joss nodded. "Great, see you in the morning." She hugged Kelly, turned and started walking towards the doors leading to the reception area.

As Kelly watched her friend leave the office, she did not notice the young investigator walk up beside her. "Who was that, Kelly?"

She spun around and glared at him. "Sod off Lee" and she walked quickly over to her new desk to continue unpacking. Diagonally opposite, the furious pen clicking seamed to be picking up speed and she groaned.

Back Lane Market Garden, Rotherham – 5:00pm Wednesday 13th May

Crosby had arrived home ten minutes earlier. He sat at the kitchen table and was just about to take a sip of steaming hot black coffee, when Caitlin's phone buzzed on the kitchen table. Until now, he had not noticed that it was there. He looked across the table at it and took a sip. The phone buzzed again and then again, and he stared at it for a couple of seconds, the mug of steaming coffee hovering just in front of his lips. The phone buzzed again.

He was curious, *who wanted to get in touch with Caitlin that much?* He put the mug down on the table and looked towards the kitchen door, to make sure that Caitlin was not in sight. He knew that he should not look at the phone, but he reached for the it anyway, his hand hovering over it as he looked towards the kitchen door again. The phone buzzed again, and he looked at it for a second more, before picking it up and tapping the screen. There was no password protection and he saw that there were four texts. He recognized the number that each one was sent from. They were from Bill Pike. He tapped on the first text and read *You were incredible the other night. Can't wait to be with you again. When can we next meet?*

Crosby read the other messages and tightened his grip on the phone. Pike had been screwing Caitlin while he was in London and the anger inside of him rose like a volcano about to explode. He jumped to his feet, toppling the chair backwards onto the floor and screamed as he threw the phone across the kitchen. It shattered against the wall by the open door. He screamed again, but louder, as he picked up the mug of coffee and threw it at the same wall. It shattered and black coffee splattered against the wall and onto the floor tiles.

He stood for a few seconds watching black coffee run down the wall and then out of the corner of his eye, he saw the notepad and pen on the worktop to his right. He grabbed them and scribbled *SCREW BILL PIKE AS MUCH AS YOU WANT TO. I NEVER WANT TO SEE YOU AGAIN.*

He slammed the notepad and pen down on the kitchen table and ran out of the kitchen and up the stairs to the bedroom. He threw open the double doors of his wardrobe and pulled an old suitcase and a leather sports bag off the top shelf. He flung the suitcase open and unzipped the sports bag. He quickly stepped over to his dresser and began stuffing pants, socks, tee-shirts, shirts and jumpers into the suitcase and the sports bag. He emptied the dresser and left the drawers in various states of open. He rushed back to the wardrobe and started throwing jeans, suits, and ties into the suitcase. He left the wardrobe doors open as he forced the suitcase and the sports bag shut.

Tears were flowing down Crosby's cheeks and he screamed. He picked up the suitcase and sports bag and ran out of the bedroom. Stumbling out of control he ran down the stairs and slammed into the empty coat stand, dropping the suitcase and sports bag. He

swore and threw the coat stand down the hallway. It landed half in the open kitchen doorway. Crosby opened the front door, picked up the suitcase and sports bag and ran across the courtyard to the barn. He threw the suitcase and bag onto the back seat of the open top TR4 and swore because he had forgotten the car keys. He sprinted back to the house. He grabbed the car keys from the bowl on the shelf above the hallway radiator, retrieved the unpacked suitcase from his trip to London and dragged it behind him as he ran out of the house, leaving the front door open. He ran as hard as he could across the courtyard to the barn and threw the suitcase into the back of the TR4 with the other suitcase and the sports bag.

He opened the driver's door and climbed into the driver's seat. Crosby slammed the door shut and started the engine. He stamped down on the clutch pedal, slammed the gearstick into reverse, let off the handbrake and reversed the car at speed out of the barn. He crunched the car into first gear, stamped down on the accelerator pedal and the wheels spun, spitting up dirt and gravel as the car sped out of the courtyard and onto the country lane.

Caitlin drove the Land Rover round a left hand bend and saw the red TR4 speeding down the lane towards her. She wondered where Crosby was going in such a hurry and flashed the Land Rover's headlights at him.

The TR4 did not slow down and as it passed by, Crosby did not acknowledge her. She saw the suitcases and sports bag on the back seat of the car and began to panic.

As Caitlin stepped through the open front door, she paused as she took in the sight of the coat stand lying half in the kitchen doorway. She walked quickly down the hallway and stepped over the coat stand. Looking around the kitchen, she took in the scene of the toppled chair, the notepad on the kitchen table and the fragments of the mug and her phone on the floor by her feet. Her heart started pounding in her chest and a new wave of panic washed over her. She forced her legs to move and she rushed over to the kitchen table. She picked up the notepad and began to read.

The notepad fell from her hand as she put it over her mouth in horror. Her knees buckled underneath her, and she slumped down onto the kitchen tiles. She began to sob uncontrollably. Crosby was an unforgiving man and she knew that her relationship with him was over.

Washington Services, Tyne & Wear – 7:45pm Wednesday 13th May

Crosby drove the TR4 into the petrol station. His back was aching from not being used to sitting in a low, small car for such a long time. He got out of the car, bent forward and touched his toes, and then stretched his arms above his head. He groaned and winced at the stiffness in his back.

He looked about the petrol station, his was the only car there. He stretched again and was reaching for the petrol pump when his phone started buzzing in his jeans pocket. He took it out and looked at the screen. The call was from the house land line, he ignored it and put the phone back into his jeans pocket. He reached for the petrol pump again and the phone buzzed again. He took the phone out of his jeans pocket and turned it off. He tossed it onto the driver's seat and opened the petrol cap on the car. Taking the pump out of its holder, he inserted the nozzle into the car, pulled the trigger on the pump and began to fill the TR4 up with petrol.

Crosby put the petrol pump back into its holder, put the petrol cap back into place and went into the shop to pay for the petrol. On his way to the counter, he picked up a bag of mints.

The young woman behind the counter smiled at

him as he approached the counter. He did not return the smile and put two twenty pound notes down on the counter. He turned and walked away, not waiting for the young woman to give him the receipt.

The young woman shouted after him. "SIR. YOUR CHANGE."

Crosby ignored her, walked out of the shop and over to the TR4. He moved his phone onto the passenger seat, got into the driver's seat and opened the bag of mints. He put two into his mouth, fastened the seatbelt and started the car. He put the gear stick into first gear, released the handbrake, pressed down hard on the accelerator pedal and the TR4 sped out of the petrol station and onto the A1M motorway heading North.

Back Lane Market Garden, Rotherham – 7:45pm Wednesday 13th May

Crosby's number was just ringing out. Caitlin screamed, pulled the phone line out of the socket in the wall and threw the phone down the hallway as hard as she could. It clattered off the half open door as it entered the kitchen. Her knees buckled underneath her and her back slid down the wall. She drew her knees up to her chest and clasped her hands around them. She began sobbing again.

The Fisherman's Rest, Alnmouth, Northumberland – 9:00pm Wednesday 13th May

Crosby had checked into his room and was sitting at the bar, nursing a pint of McEwan's Best Scotch. He looked around the room and all about him were people laughing and in deep conversation. He suddenly felt very lonely. He sighed and his shoulders slumped. He put the glass of beer down on the bar and took his phone out of his jeans pocket. He switched it on and checked for any missed calls. There were non. He sent a text to Kelly Mathers saying *What time do you arrive? I'll pick you up at the station. Joe.*

He put the phone down on the bar and as he reached for the pint glass, his phone buzzed. He picked it up and read the text @ *11:30 c u then. Kelly x.*

He put the phone back into his jeans pocket, picked up the pint glass and drained it. He looked around the bar again, the same laughter and conversations. He shook his head and as he put the glass back down on the bar, a familiar voice from over his right shoulder said, "Hello bonny lad?"

Crosby turned on the bar stool and forced a smile. "Maggie, it's great to see you. It's been a while?" He slipped off the bar stool and gave the landlady a hug, lifting her off her feet.

"It's good to see you Joe. Sorry I wasn't here when you checked in. I was visiting old Billy Wright down the road. His arthritis has been playing up."

"That's okay, Maggie."

The landlady smiled. "Buy me a drink and we'll have a good old catch-up."

Crosby was still smiling. "Gin and orange, is it?"

"Yes, please. A large one."

Crosby ordered the gin and orange and a pint of McEwan's Best Scotch, and the landlady hitched herself up onto the bar stool beside him. She gently tapped him on the knee. "Now, tell me what's been going on with you."

Crosby said, "Thanks," to the barman and handed the landlady her drink. He forced a smile. "You're looking good, Maggie."

The landlady shook her head.

"What?"

"Joe, I've known you for too long to not know when you're running away from something. What's going on pet?"

Crosby took a long drink of beer, a deep breath and began telling the landlady how his world had been turned upside down just six days ago with the reappearance of Bill Pike in his life.

2:00am Thursday 14th May

Bright moonlight streamed through the gap in the curtains and Crosby could not sleep. He had been tossing and turning all night and now he was staring at the ceiling in the attic bedroom. He reached for his phone on the bedside table, looked at the time, sighed loudly and decided to go for a walk. He pulled the duvet back and swung his legs out of bed, his feet sinking into the deep pile carpet. He reached for his jeans from the chair beside the bedside table, stood up and pulled them on. He dressed quickly, pushing his sockless feet into soft, brown leather shoes and left the room as he was pulling on an old, faded, blue hoody.

He pulled down the peak of an old, grey baseball cap as he quietly walked down the landing, descended the stairs and walked across the bar to the door. As he unlocked the door, a voice said, "Can't sleep bonny lad?" He paused but did not turn around. He opened the door, stepped out into the warm night air and closed the door quietly behind him.

Crosby stood for a moment and breathed in a big lungful of the night air. He listened, and all was quiet except for the sound of lapping waves on the nearby coastline. He turned to his right and began walking down the empty street. With every step, the sound of gently lapping water got louder, as he got closer to the mouth of the River Aln. He walked past two wooden benches, down a sandy track and onto the sand dunes.

Crosby stood on top of a sand dune, his feet slowly sinking and his shoes filling up with sand. He did not care and pushed his hands into his jeans pockets, raised his chin and closed his eyes. The night was silent. The warm coastal breeze caressed his face and the sound of lapping water brought a calm to his life that he liked.

After a long few seconds, he opened his eyes and looked across the river mouth and out to the North Sea. He realized he was smiling and that in the moment, he was at peace and happy.

Out of the corner of his eye, Crosby saw a figure walking across the dunes towards him. He stood with his hands in his pockets and watched the woman get closer. She was slim and wearing a white top under an unzipped bodywarmer, skintight jeans tucked into calf length boots and her blonde hair was tied back in a ponytail. She was beautiful, and he could not take his eyes off her.

When the woman was only a couple of feet away from him, he greeted her with a touch of the peak of his baseball cap. She smiled softly and said, "Hi. Joe."

A tear rolled down his face as he smiled back and said quietly, "Hello Rosie."

She stood beside him, turning to look out across the river mouth, not saying a word.

Crosby forced himself to look away from her. He looked back out across the river mouth and closed his eyes for a moment. When he opened them, Rosie was gone. Silent tears rolled down his cheeks and he did not bother to wipe them away. He whispered, "I love you," and thought he heard on the warm night breeze, Rosie say, "I love you too, Joe."

Alnmouth station - 11:35am Thursday 14th May

As the train to Edinburgh pulled into the station, Crosby got out of the TR4. Not many passengers got off the train, so it was easy to see Kelly walking towards him, pulling her suitcase behind her. He waved and as he watched her walking towards him, he noticed her short, red hair, bright in the morning sunlight. The light grey, fitted, business suit she was wearing accentuated the curve of her hips, and the two inch heels made her look tall and elegant.

She greeted him with a smile. "Hello, Joe."

He smiled back. "Hi."

She nodded towards the open top TR4. "Nice car."

Crosby grinned and ran his right hand lightly over the bright red paintwork. "Thanks. It's a classic."

Kelly left her suitcase and walked slowly around the car, letting her fingers run lightly over the polished paintwork as she went.

Crosby watched her intently.

A smile spread across Kelly's face and as she neared Crosby she said, "It's a very nice car, Joe."

Crosby was still grinning. He stepped over to Kelly's suitcase and put it on the back seat. "I thought that I'd get you checked in and then take you out for the day, to show you the beautiful Northumberland coastline."

"You've been here before?"

Crosby nodded. "Yes. Me and Rosie used to come up here a lot."

Kelly smiled. "Oh. Okay. Let's go then" and she got into the passenger seat of the sports car.

Crosby got into the driver's seat and started the car. The engine purred. He fastened his seatbelt, put the car into first gear and grinning, said, "Hang on." He released the handbrake and pressed down hard on the accelerator pedal. The wheels spun and the TR4 sped out of the station carpark.

The Fisherman's Rest, Alnmouth - 12:00pm Thursday 14th May

Crosby put Kelly's suitcase down on the floor between them and leaned against the bar.

The landlady smiled. "Hello Joe. And you must be Joe's work mate, Kelly Mathers."

Crosby made the introductions. "Kelly, this is Maggie Swan. She owns the place."

Kelly held her hand out for a handshake. "I'm pleased to meet you."

The landlady was still smiling as she lightly shook Kelly's hand. "It's nice to finally meet you."

As Kelly let go from the handshake, she looked at Crosby, her eyes narrowing and her head slightly to one side. She was confused. "Finally meet me? I don't understand?"

Crosby put his hands deep into his jeans pockets, looked down at his boots and shifted his weight from his left leg to his right. "Maggie is Rosie's mother."

Kelly was stunned at that piece of information and her head whipped back to look at Maggie. "Oh. I see."

The landlady was still smiling. "Rosie mentioned you a lot. She used to say that you were Joe's other woman."

Kelly was still confused. "But Joe and I have never......"

Crosby cut in. "You were my secretary for a lot of years, Kelly. You ran my professional life and Rosie ran my personal life."

"Oh! I see," and Kelly started laughing. When she had finished, she said, "I get it, sorry for being so slow on the uptake."

The landlady came out from behind the bar. "Follow me pet, I'll show you up to your room. You're next to Joe."

Kelly picked up her suitcase and followed the landlady through the bar.

Crosby called after them. "I'll get the drinks in."

The landlady opened the bedroom door and let Kelly walk in first. She scanned the room, nicely made up double bed, bedside table and lamp, pine dresser and wardrobe and coastal scene paintings on each wall. She turned to the landlady and smiled. "I like the paintings."

"Rosie painted them when she was at school. When she was in sixth form I think."

Kelly stepped closer to the painting with the castle on the headland. "It's very good."

The landlady looked around the room at the paintings and smiled as happy memories came flooding back of the days when Rosie would come home with a new painting. A tear trickled down her cheek and she quickly wiped it away. "She was a good artist. She loved painting the Northumberland coast. Did you know that she had a BA honors Art degree from Edinburgh University?"

Kelly shook her head. "No, I didn't." She walked over to the window. It looked out over the other properties close by.

The landlady joined her. "Sorry. There's no sea view, but it's a nice comfortable room."

Kelly turned and smiled. That's okay and I do like the room,"

The landlady indicated with her right hand. "The bathroom's just through there pet. I change the towels every day."

Kelly walked into the bathroom, nodded her approval at the long, deep bath with a shower overhead and walked out to the bed. She sat down. "The room's lovely, Mrs. Swan."

The landlady waved her hand and dismissed the formality. "Please. All of Rosie and Joe's friends call me Maggie."

Kelly smiled and nodded. "I didn't know Rosie was a northern girl. She didn't have an accent."

The landlady let out a short laugh. "That's because she used to say it was hard enough being a woman in the investigations game, without people thinking she was a thick northerner too."

Kelly let out a short laugh. "She's right about it being hard for women. In the ten years that I worked for Brightside as a secretary, Rosie was the only female investigator they ever hired."

The landlady continued. "Joe used to call Rosie, Miss Jekyll, because she was one person at work and a totally different person when she was here at home."

A tear rolled down Kelly's cheek. She dug a tissue out of her bag and dabbed it away. "I would have liked to have known the other Rosie."

The landlady sat down on the bed next to Kelly and gently patted her leg. "You would have liked the other Rosie, my Rosie."

Kelly sniffed and dabbed the corner of her eyes with the tissue. "Sorry."

"That's okay pet" and the landlady stood up. "Shall we go back down to Joe, have lunch and a couple of drinks?"

Kelly sniffed and nodded. She rose from the bed and followed the landlady out of the room, closing the door behind her.

Craster, Northumberland - 6:00pm Thursday 14th May

The TR4 was parked facing towards the small harbour and the North Sea. Crosby put a chip into his mouth and licked his fingers.

Kelly was looking out to sea. "What do you call this place again?"

"Craster."

Kelly nodded and put a chip into her mouth.

A long silence descended on the small sports car as they ate their fish and chips and looked out over the harbour.

Kelly broke the silence. "Thank you for today. I never knew that the North East was so beautiful."

Crosby turned to her. "You've never been up here before?"

Kelly shook her head. "No. I'm a London girl and except for a few holidays down in Brighton, I've never been anywhere."

Crosby nodded, stuffed a piece of fish into his mouth and turned back to the harbour.

Kelly continued. "I like it here though."

Crosby kept his eyes on the harbour. "Me too," he said quietly.

Kelly put a piece of fish into her mouth and closed her eyes as she chewed slowly. She savoured the taste and the warm, evening breeze from the sea on her face. She was far away from the hustle, noise and grime of London and she sighed, letting her shoulders relax. She was happy.

Crosby screwed the remnants of his fish and chips up in the paper and said, "We'll go and see Robert Grant's wife tomorrow morning, at her shop in Alnwick.

Kelly opened her eyes and turned to Crosby. "Why are we seeing her alone?"

Crosby continued to look out over the harbour. "I want to ask her about how she felt when Robert and not William, asked her to marry him."

Kelly thought for a moment. "That's an awkward question to answer in front of your husband."

"Exactly and if Robert was present, I doubt that we'd get a truthful answer."

Kelly nodded.

Crosby continued "I want you to watch her body language very carefully and tell me what your woman's intuition thinks."

Kelly screwed her fish and chip paper up noisily. "That's a sexist thing to say. Woman's intuition."

Crosby instantly knew from Kelly's tone that he was on shaky ground. He turned to her and put his hands up in defence. "Sorry. I didn't mean it like that. It's just that ….."

Kelly cut him off and she was grinning. "I know what you meant. I'm just pulling your chain."

Crosby grunted and turned back to the harbour. "Okay," he said flatly.

Kelly took the screwed up fish and chip paper

from the dashboard in front of Crosby and put it in the nearby bin with her own paper.

Crosby watched her walk to and from the bin and thought to himself, *She's a beautiful lady.*

Alnwick, Northumberland - 11:30am Friday 15th May

Crosby stopped at the door to the small art shop and turned to Kelly. "This is it. We'll pretend we're browsing to buy and let Anna Grant approach us."

Kelly glanced into the shop through the door glass and let out a short exhale of breath. "Okay."

Crosby smiled at her. "You'll do great," and he opened the door. He stepped aside for Kelly to enter first.

Kelly winked at him. "Such a gentleman," and stepped through the doorway.

Crosby grinned and followed her into the shop, closing the door behind him. He quickly scanned the shop and recognized Anna Grant from the photographs in the files. She was sitting behind an ultra-modern, glass-topped desk to his right and was thumbing through a magazine. Her light ginger hair was styled neatly into a plait and shone bright against her pale complexion. She was wearing a pearl necklace and matching earrings, which complemented the cream, soft wool V-neck sweater she was wearing.

Out of the corner of her left eye, Kelly saw a flash of red and she instinctively moved left towards it. She walked over to a large oil painting depicting a woman wearing a red raincoat, walking down a cobbled, dimly lit street at night.

Crosby joined Kelly at her left shoulder and whispered into her ear, "If we linger long enough at each painting, it will look like we're serious buyers."

Kelly nodded her head very slightly and took hold of Crosby's hand, to make it look like they were a couple.

Crosby whispered again, "Holding hands, a nice touch."

After fifteen minutes of watching the couple move around the shop, Anna Grant decided it was time to introduce herself and to make a sale. She rose from her chair behind the desk and walked over to them. She arrived wearing her best smile. "Good morning. I'm Anna, owner of the shop. This is a fine piece indeed. It was painted by James Marshall, a local artist from Amble. He captures the full moon on the water beautifully, don't you think?"

Kelly turned and smiled. "He does, I like it. But I prefer the painting with the lady in the red raincoat."

Anna turned to the paining. "Ah. Yes. It is one of my favourite pieces. It is by a Cumbrian artist called Alistair Brice. He's captured beautifully the sense that the woman is hurrying to the warmth and comfort of her home after a night out with friends."

Kelly turned to the painting and nodded. "My thoughts exactly," and a smile spread across her face. She was enjoying playing the part of Ms Couple browsing to buy art for her house.

Crosby saw a twinkle in Kelly's eye and smiled. He turned to Anna Grant and cut into the conversation. "Mrs. Grant, we're here...."

"I'll take it."

"Crosby whipped his head around to look at Kelly. "What?"

"The painting. I'll take it." Kelly squeezed Crosby's hand and dragged him a few feet away from Anna. She kept her voice very low, almost a whisper, "I genuinely want the painting and if I buy from her, I think she's more likely to be receptive to answering our questions. Now kiss me and smile."

Crosby lowered his voice to the same level as Kelly's. "On the lips?"

Kelly smiled.

Crosby gently placed both hands on Kelly's face and kissed her softly on the lips.

Kelly instinctively put both hands on Crosby's waist, closed her eyes and responded. After a couple of seconds, she gently pushed herself away from Crosby, turned to Anna and smiled. "I'll take the painting. Thank you."

Anna Grant nodded and smiled. She walked over to the painting, took it off the wall and carried it over to her desk for wrapping.

Crosby watched Anna Grant's hands dance over the thick, brown wrapping paper as she folded it over the painting. On her long, thin fingers she wore a three diamond engagement ring, a thin gold wedding band and a ruby and diamond eternity ring, and Crosby tried to estimate the value of the jewelry on one finger alone.

Just as Kelly was taking back her credit card from Anna Grant, Crosby spoke. "Mrs. Grant, we're actually here to talk to you about the disappearance of William Grant."

Anna Grant stopped smiling and what little colour she had in her cheeks drained away. She crossed her arms and looked Crosby dead in the eye. "I don't know anything about that. I can't help you. I'm sorry."

Kelly smiled softly. "Lord and Lady Grant are very worried about William and have asked us to find him. Any scrap of information might lead to a breakthrough in finding him."

Crosby smiled and thought to himself, *She's a natural at this.*

Anna Grant un-crossed her arms and studied the rings on her wedding finger. She turned the wedding band around on her finger and sighed. She did not look up. "About eighteen months ago, William turned up at the house unexpectedly. He gave no explanation for his visit and he didn't stay very long. When we got up the next morning, he was gone."

Crosby nodded. "He stayed only one night?"

"Yes."

Kelly cut in "What did you talk about while he was staying with you?"

Anna Grant still played with the rings and she shook her head. "We didn't talk. I showed him up to the guest room and left him there. He never came out of the room and as I have already told you, he had left by the time we got up the next morning."

Watching and listening to Kelly, Crosby decided that she stood the best chance of getting as much information out of Anna Grant as possible, so he turned and walked away towards the back of the shop. He heard her say, "What time did you wake up?"

"About eight thirty, I think."

"And William didn't leave a note?"

Anna shook her head. "No. He came and went without saying a word to me or Robert."

Kelly smiled across the desk at Anna. "This is very helpful Mrs. Grant, thank you."

Anna smiled thinly and some colour returned to her cheeks.

Crosby returned to the desk. "William and Robert are twins and look alike?"

Anna Grant folded her arms and sighed loudly. "Yes."

"How do you tell them apart?"

Anna turned to Kelly. "I don't see how this is relevant to finding William."

Kelly smiled. "Please. Any small bit of information can help, no matter how irrelevant it may seem."

Anna Grant sighed loudly again "Okay. They each have a small freckle above opposite eyebrows."

Kelly nodded. "Thank you. Which eyebrow is your husband's freckle above?"

Without hesitation, Anna said "His left eyebrow."

Kelly smiled. "Thank you."

Crosby continued the questioning. "Lord and Lady Grant said that you and William were very close. How did you feel when Robert proposed to you?"

Anna Grant glared at Crosby, she clenched her hands into fists and raised her voice. "Really! How is this relevant to finding William?"

Kelly tried to diffuse the situation. "Please believe me Mrs. Grant, it does help. You're being very helpful and we're very grateful for you time."

Another loud sigh. "Very well. I was surprised

and disappointed, but William had given me no indication that he wanted to get married. I loved Robert, but not in the same way as I love William. I thought, why not marry Robert, maybe I could love him in the same way as I do William. So, I said yes."

Kelly smiled. "And, do you?"

"Do I what?"

"Do you love your husband in the same way as you love William?"

"Yes. I do. Of course I do." Anna snapped and banged her fist down on the desk. She glared at Crosby. "Now, if you don't mind, I have things to do and I would like you to leave now."

Kelly picked up the painting, wrapped neatly in thick brown paper and fastened with string. She smiled at Anna Grant. "Thank you for your time and help Mrs. Grant and I really do love the painting."

Crosby and Kelly walked towards the shop door and Anna Grant followed them to make sure that they actually left the premises.

At the door, Crosby turned to Anna Grant. "Thank you again for your time and patience Mrs. Grant, you have been very helpful." He dug into the right inside pocket of his suit jacket and pulled out a business card. He held it out for Anna Grant to take from him. "If you think of anything that might help us find William, please call me."

Anna Grant snatched the card out of Crosby's hand, opened the door and indicated with her free hand for them to leave. The look on her face said *leave and never come back.*

Crosby and Kelly stepped out onto the street and into the warm afternoon sunshine. The door slammed shut behind them and the loud click of the lock made sure that they could not re-enter the shop.

As they walked up the street, Kelly said, "Did you notice that she said she loved Robert, but not in the same way as I love William."

Crosby stopped and turned to Kelly. "She still loves him?"

"Yes."

Crosby shook his head. "I'm out of practice, I missed that."

They continued to walk up the street and Crosby started to mull over that Anna Grant was still in love with her husband's brother.

Crosby and Kelly walked to the TR4 in silence. Crosby paused as he was about to open the driver's door. "Do you think it's strange that when William turned up at the house, that she never spoke to him, the man she's still in love with, even if he was only there a very short time?"

Kelly put the painting on the back seat of the car. She nodded. "Yes. And I don't believe her." She opened the passenger side door, got into the car and pulled the door shut.

Crosby got into the driver's seat, slammed the door shut and started the car. He turned to Kelly. "We'll pay the Grant's a surprise visit tonight and see what Robert Grant has to say about his brother's surprise visit."

Kelly turned to Crosby. "Anna's not going to be happy about that."

Crosby shrugged. "I don't care" and putting the car into first gear and releasing the handbrake, he pressed down on the accelerator and carefully drove the TR4 out of the tight parking space.

The Fisherman's Rest, Alnmouth - 1:00pm Friday 15th May

Crosby was raising a pint of McEwans Best Scotch to his lips, just as his phone buzzed and did a little dance on the table. He stared at it for a long few seconds and took a long drink.

Kelly looked at the phone and then at Crosby. "Are you not going to read the text?"

"It's from my sister, I'll read it later."

Kelly stared at Crosby and took a mouthful of cider.

"What?" Crosby snapped.

"You should read it. It might be important."

"It's not."

"How do you know it's not important, you've not read it."

Crosby shook his head and sighed loudly. He took another long swallow of beer.

Kelly was just about to say something more about the text, when Crosby was saved by the waitress arriving at the table with their food.

Kelly looked up, smiled and said, "Thank you."

The young waitress smiled back. "Enjoy your meals."

Crosby put a slice of cucumber into his mouth and looked up at Kelly, who was staring at him. He shrugged. "What?"

Kelly nodded at the phone. "Read it."

Crosby sighed again, picked up the phone and read the text. He put the phone back down on to the table without saying a word.

"Well?" Kelly demanded.

"It's not important."

Kelly saw a flash of pain in Crosby's eyes. She did not believe him, and she snatched up the phone and read the text. She glared at Crosby as she put the phone back down onto the table, "Bullshit, it's not important. Caitlin has left you."

Crosby took another long drink of beer, "Good riddance and by the way, I left her."

Kelly waited for more.

Crosby drained the pint. "She slept with Bill Pike and I told her not to be at home when I got back."

Kelly tried to say something, but no words came. She cut into the omelette on the plate in front of her and said, "Sorry" as she raised the fork to her mouth.

Crosby forced a smile across the table at her. "Don't be sorry, it's fine," and he put a cherry tomato into his mouth.

Brightside Investigations, Chancery Lane, London - 4:00pm Friday 15th May

Bill Pike suddenly sat up and looked around the office. He rubbed his face and spoke to himself into his hands. "Fuck! I must have dozed off."

He was just about to shout for his secretary to bring him a strong coffee when his phone buzzed on the desk beside his laptop. He picked it up and tapped the screen. It was a text from Caitlin saying *Meet me at Cleopatra's needle on Victoria Embankment at 9 2nite.*

Pike smiled to himself, put the phone down and shouted, "Joss, a strong coffee please."

He rubbed his face again, put on his glasses and leaned forward in his chair to read the billing report on his laptop screen, which had made him doze off in the first place.

The Old Rectory, Howick, Northumberland - 7:00pm Friday 15th May

The old, oak door creaked loudly as Anna Grant opened it. She took half a step backwards, surprised to see Crosby and Kelly standing in front of her. "What.... You.... What are you doing here?"

Crosby smiled. "We'd like to ask your husband some questions about the night William turned up here unexpectedly."

Kelly stepped up onto the bottom step. "Mrs. Grant, any little piece of information from your husband might lead us to find William."

Anna Grant thought for a moment, nodded, and opened the door wide for Crosby and Kelly to enter the house. It creaked again. "Robert's in the study. First door on the left."

Kelly smiled and said "Thank you" as she stepped into the house.

Crosby nodded his thanks, stepped through the doorway and quickly scanned the hallway and the old staircase to his right.

Crosby walked into the study and immediately the heat of the room hit him. He felt the soft, thick pile of the carpet underfoot and quickly scanned the room, an old wooden desk with a laptop on it at the far end of the room and a landscape oil painting on the paneled wall behind it, bookshelves stuffed with books covering the whole of the wall by the door, four lamps on tables scattered about the room and two old, red leather chairs either side of the wood burner.

Robert Grant was sitting in the chair to the left of the wood burner reading a paperback book. He dabbed at his forehead with a white cotton handkerchief.

Crosby put on a smile and stepped towards Grant's chair. He held out his hand for a handshake. "I'm Joe Crosby and this is my associate, Kelly Mathers. We work for Brightside Investigations and have been engaged by Lord and Lady Grant to find your brother, William."

Grant rose from the chair and firmly shook the offered hand. "Robert Grant. Pleased to meet you."

Kelly smiled and nodded to Grant.

Grant ignored Kelly and sat back down in the chair. He did not offer Crosby or Kelly a seat. "How can I help you Mr. Crosby?"

Crosby put his hands into his suit trouser pockets, "You told the previous investigators that William left before daybreak and that his bed had not been slept in."

"Yes. That's correct."

"Did you go into his room to see if he was there?"

Grant shook his head. "No. Anna did. She said that his bed had not been slept in."

Crosby nodded. "I see. Did you not hear him leave? That's a creaky, old front door you have there."

Grant thought for a moment. "You know, I'm a heavy sleeper. I thought I heard footsteps and the door, but I thought I must have been dreaming. In fact, the door's only been creaking like that recently and I really must have it fixed soon. "

Kelly cut in. "You didn't get up to investigate?"

"No."

Crosby smiled. "Thank you, Mr. Grant" and he turned to leave the room.

As Crosby reached the door, he stopped and turned back to Robert Grant. "Why did William come here? Did he say?"

Grant shook his head and shrugged. "I don't know. He didn't say."

Kelly cut in. "Did you speak with your brother?"

Grant shook his head again. "No."

Crosby spoke, "One last question Mr. Grant. How far is the coastal path from the back of your house?"

Grant dabbed at his forehead with the handkerchief. "Not far. Five minutes if you walk across a couple of fields and climb over the dry stone wall."

Crosby smiled and nodded. "Thank you for your time Mr. Grant." He turned and left the room.

Kelly smiled and nodded her thanks and followed Crosby out of the room.

Crosby and Kelly stood on the coastal path, looking out over the North Sea.

"Joe, why did you want to come out here? You think William was pushed over the cliff?" Kelly laughed.

Crosby turned slightly to his right and looked Kelly dead in the eye. "It's a possibility." He turned back to the sea. "Did you notice how old the staircase was?"

Kelly shook her head. "No."

"It's old and I'll bet that it creaks with every step you take up or down it."

Kelly thought for a long few seconds. "So, if the staircase creaks and if the front door creaked, you think there's no way that Anna or Robert would not have heard William leaving in the middle of the night."

Crosby turned back to Kelly. "Exactly. "

Kelly thought for a moment. "What if William went out of the back door? We don't know if that door creaks like the front door."

Crosby smiled. "It doesn't matter, I don't believe that anyone could get down that staircase quietly. My gut is telling me that something happened to William Grant that night."

Kelly turned to look back out to sea and began to think *Okay, William was followed down the stairs and out of the house. But why would he come to the coastal path and why would his brother push him over the cliff edge?* She sighed as she tried to think through the puzzle.

After a few minutes of silence, Crosby asked "Do you think it's strange that the Grants had the wood burner on in the middle of May and that Robert Grant was sitting so close to it. It's not a cold night at all."

Kelly turned slightly to Crosby. "People with circulation problems feel the cold. Maybe Robert Grant has circulation problems."

Cosby nodded. "How did Robert Grant seem to you?"

"He appeared confident, but I think he was nervous. He was sweating."

"That wood burner made the room very warm."

"Maybe. And I'm sure he was wearing makeup."

Crosby turned to her. "Makeup?"

Kelly nodded. "Yes. He was sweating and dabbing at his forehead with that handkerchief. I swear it had makeup on it."

"You saw the freckle over his left eyebrow?"

"Yes. What are you thinking, Joe?"

Crosby shook his head. "I don't know. Something's not right, I just can't put my finger on it."

There was a couple of minutes silence and Crosby broke it. "Right, that's enough for the day, let's go." As he turned, he hesitated and stared south down the path.

Kelly followed his gaze. "What is it, Joe?"

"You see that man over there?"

"Yes."

"He's just standing there looking at us."

Kelly shrugged. "So what?"

Crosby did not answer. He stared at the man, who turned and started walking away.

Crosby tugged Kelly's arm. "Come on. Let's see what he wants," and he set off down the path.

Crosby knocked on the old farm cottage door and a voice shouted, "COME IN."

The door was unlocked, and Crosby pushed it open. It creaked. He stepped into a small, stone flagged kitchen with whitewashed stone walls and warm evening light shining through small, dirty windows. He scanned the room, open fireplace with an old rocking chair just to the right side of it, an old table and two un-matching chairs by a window and an old dresser with some crockery on it. The room was sparse but clean.

A man, about six feet tall with grey cropped hair and wearing old army issue fatigues and boots, was standing at the sink scrubbing his hands in an old, deep, ceramic sink. He did not look at Crosby and Kelly or say anything.

Crosby coughed to clear his throat. "I'm Joe Crosby and this is my associate, Kelly Mathers. We work for Brightside Investigations."

The man did not look up or answer and continued to scrub his hands.

Crosby continued. "I saw you on the coastal path and got the feeling that you wanted to talk to us."

The man still did not answer. He took his hands out of the soapy water, shook them and turned them over. He inspected his hands closely, "Got to get the blood off my hands, you see." He nodded his satisfaction and dried his hands on a rag, which was on the wooden worktop next to the sink. He turned towards Crosby and studied him for a few seconds. His gaze turned from Crosby to Kelly and he looked her over from head to toe.

Kelly forced a smile. The man's gaze made her feel a little uncomfortable and she looked down at her feet.

The man leaned back against the worktop and waited for Crosby or Kelly to speak.

Crosby looked around the room and noticed on the mantle over the fire, a faded photograph of soldiers wearing maroon berets and holding a union flag. He nodded towards it. "Are you in that photograph?"

The man turned towards the photograph and smiled. "Yes. A good day that was." He walked towards the fireplace and picked the photograph up. His smile spread further across his face.

Crosby needed to keep the conversation going, he did not want to lose the man in his memories. "When was it taken?"

"The day we liberated Port Stanley from the Argies."

Crosby asked, "You were in the parachute regiment?"

The man nodded and did not take his eyes off the photograph. "Three para."

Crosby grimaced. "Mount Longdon, the bloodiest battle of the war."

The man's face went blank and he did not answer.

Kelly walked over to the man and lightly put her hand on his shoulder. "What's your name?"

The man snapped out of his daydream. "Terry Creighton."

Kelly smiled. "I'm Kelly. Could I please see the photograph?"

Creighton nodded.

Kelly took the photograph from him and looked closely at it for a few seconds. "What's the soldier in the background doing? The one bending down?"

Creighton smiled. "That's a kid from B Company's rifle company giving a little lad his beret. He had a really bad time up on the mountain. He just about survived."

Crosby cut in. "Is there something you wanted to tell us Mr. Creighton?"

Creighton nodded towards the table and two chairs. "Have a seat."

Crosby sat down, and Kelly put the photograph back onto the mantle above the fireplace. She stayed by the fireplace.

Creighton cleared his throat and a rasp came from his chest. "I go for walks. I have to you see, to calm my nerves. Sometimes I go out in the middle of the night. I have to stay awake as much as I can to keep the nightmares of Mount Longdon away."

Creighton looked down, started picking at his fingernails and drifted off into his nightmare.

After a long minute's silence, Crosby brought Creighton back to reality. "Terry, can I call you Terry?"

Creighton looked up. "Yes."

Crosby smiled. "Please go on Terry."

Creighton nodded. "Sorry. Drifted off for a moment. Anyway, I saw you come out of the Grants' house and from the way you were talking on the path, I wondered if you were the police."

Kelly cut in. "Is there something you think the police should know?"

Creighton nodded. "About eighteen months ago, I was having really bad nightmares and was going out walking along the coast path at all hours of the night. In the early hours of...... a day in November I think, it was blowing a gale, the worst there's been since I've lived here, I saw a small light moving from the old rectory, across the fields to the coast path. I thought it was Mr. Grant with the torch but then I saw a man following him who looked just like him. They could have been brothers I suppose. I didn't know Mr. Grant......."

Crosby interrupted. "You must have been close?"

Creighton nodded. "About ten feet away, I was crouched down very still in the shadow of the wall while they were talking."

Crosby nodded.

Creighton continued. "They were standing right where you were standing. At first everything was okay between them and then the man with the torch said he loved....... Annie, I think."

Kelly piped up. "Anna?"

Creighton nodded. "Yes, Anna. Mr. Grant's wife. Anyway, they started arguing and the man with the torch punched the other man. He clocked him right up by the temple and he fell to the ground. He didn't seem to move after that."

Creighton shook his head and stared at the stone floor. He came back to the present when Kelly said, "Terry?"

Creighton looked up and continued. "Sorry. I drift off sometimes. I got blown off my feet by an Argie artillery shell when we were dug in on Mount London. Lost my helmet and hit my head on a rock. The doc said it scrambled my brain a little bit."

Kelly smiled. "That's okay Terry. Please go on."

Creighton smiled back. "Okay. The man with the torch started pacing up and down, like he was trying to work out what to do with the other man. I didn't want to find out, so I used the noise of the wind and the sea crashing against the rocks to creep away."

Crosby nodded. "I see. Do you know what happened to the man on the ground?"

Creighton shook his head. "No. I didn't look

back and I came straight home."

Crosby stood up. "Thank you, Terry. You've been very helpful."

Kelly followed Crosby to the door and smiled her thanks just before she stepped out into the warm night air.

After five minutes of walking back along the coastal path towards the Grants' house, Kelly said, "I think Terry Creighton has just described a murder to us."

Crosby stopped. "Possibly. First thing tomorrow morning, call Ken Williams at the office and ask him to make enquiries with the parachute regiment about Mr. Creighton. The battle for Mount Longdon was hand to hand combat and was the bloodiest battle of the Falklands war, so I'm not surprised that he has nightmares. He said himself, that his brain is a bit scrambled, so let's see if the paras have any record of him having any psychological problems associated with hallucinations as a result of his experiences in the Falklands war."

Kelly nodded. "Okay."

Victoria Embankment, London – 9:00pm Friday 15th May

Caitlin stood under a tree, across the road from Cleopatra's Needle, watching for Pike to arrive. She checked for the tenth time that her hair was tucked up into the faded New York Yankees baseball cap and pulled down on the peak, to make sure that it partially hid her face. She looked left and then right across the road and saw Pike approaching the monument. He was walking at a comfortable pace, his hands in his suit trouser pockets. He looked relaxed. She smiled.

Pike stopped about ten feet away from the monument and scanned the immediate area around him for Caitlin. He could not see her. He checked his watch. He was on time and she was late. He frowned. He scanned the area again for her, sighed and walked to the monument. He moved to his right and around the monument to the riverside. He stood with his hands in his pockets, looking out over the Thames and waited for Caitlin to arrive.

Caitlin watched Pike walk round to the river side of the monument. She just needed the crowd by the monument to thin out and then she would make her move. She dug some cheap, thick rimmed glasses out of a side pocket of the combat jacket she was wearing, put them on to disguise her face, and checked again, that her hair was tucked under the baseball cap. She continued to lean against the tree trunk and watched the crowd.

Pike checked his watch again. Caitlin was five minutes late. He swore and immediately apologised to the elderly American couple who looked at him with disgust. The couple moved on without a word and he swore again.

The crowd around the monument started to thin out and suddenly, it seemed that Pike would be alone. Caitlin made her move. She quickly walked across the road and as she stepped onto the pavement, she pulled a thin, six-inch blade out of a deep side pocket in the combat jacket. The air cushion soles of her new trainers made no sound on the stone floor as she came up behind Pike and with as much strength as she could muster, she stabbed the blade into the side of Pike's neck. At the same time, she used her left forearm and her body weight to push him over the low wall and into the fast flowing river.

Pike instinctively grabbed for the knife as he tumbled head first towards the dirty water.

Caitlin did not wait to hear the splash of Pike's body hitting the water. She quickly turned away, stuffed her hands into the combat jacket's pockets and joined the foot traffic passing the monument. She was calm, her breathing was normal, and her walking pace was relaxed. She did not look back.

Pike pulled the blade out of his neck just before he hit the water. Blood spurted out of the wound and then he was under the water. He let go of the blade as he instinctively put his hand over the wound, which made it more difficult to fight the strong under current dragging him further under the water and away from the riverbank. He fought for breath and wildly kicked his legs to try and reach the surface. It was a futile effort. He tried to scream but his mouth filled with dirty river water. He stopped kicking, closed his eyes and let himself be dragged down into the darkness of the river.

Caitlin crossed over the road, entered the tube station and headed for the ladies' toilets. She pushed the door open and was relieved to find that she was alone. She quickly took off the glasses, baseball cap and combat jacket. She put the glasses in the bin and hung the jacket and baseball cap on a peg on the door of the toilet stall at the far end of the room. She went over to one of the sinks, turned on the cold water tap and washed her hands and face. She dried them with paper towels, ran her fingers through her hair to make it look presentable and smiled at herself in the mirror. She took a deep breath, turned and left the toilets, joining the crowd in the busy tube station.

The Fisherman's Rest, Alnmouth - 10:00pm Friday 15th May

Crosby sat down on the bed, kicked off his shoes and rubbed his face. He was tired and yawned. His phone buzzed on the bed beside him, the screen showing that it was Sally calling.

He groaned, picked up the phone and answered without any enthusiasm. "Hi Sally. It's late."

"Joe, you haven't answered my texts."

"Crosby said nothing.

"Joe, Caitlin's disappeared."

"I don't care."

"What's happened, Joe?"

Crosby sighed. "I'm tired Sally. I don't want to talk about this right now."

There was a long minute's silence and Sally broke it. "Joe, what's happened? Are you all right? I'm worried about you."

Crosby was slumped forward with silent tears rolling down his face. His voice quivered, "Caitlin slept with Bill Pike." He heard Sally's sharp intake of breath.

"I...... I don't know what to say, Joe."

Crosby shook his head and a tear dripped off the end of his nose. His voice was shaky, "After Rosie, I really thought Caitlin was the girl for me. I was even thinking about asking her to marry me after this job is finished."

Sally shook her head and began crying for her brother. Through her tears, she managed to say, "Oh, Joe. I'm so sorry."

Crosby wiped his tears away with the back of his hand and sniffed. "Sally, it's because of Bill that I've lost Rosie and now Caitlin. I'll kill the bastard the next time I see him."

Before Sally could say another word, Crosby ended the call and switched his phone off. The phone slid out of his hand and onto the floor and he slumped back onto the bed. He pulled his knees up to his chest and began crying uncontrollably.

8:15am Saturday 16ᵗʰ May

Kelly walked over to the window in her room and looked out at the surrounding houses. The sun was shining and as it streamed through the window, she savoured its warmth on her face. A smile spread across her face and she tapped the 'call' button on the phone screen.

The call was answered on the second ring. "Brightside Investigations, Ken Williams speaking."

"Good morning, Mr. Williams, it's Kelly Mathers."

"Hello Kelly and you can stop calling me Mr. Williams. You're an investigator now, so you can call me Ken."

Kelly turned away from the window and sat on the bed. "Oh! Okay. Good morning……Ken."

"That's better. Now, what do I owe the pleasure of such an early call on a Saturday?"

"Could you check with the parachute regiment to see if a former member of the third battalion, Terry Creighton, had any history of psychological problems associated with hallucinations after he came back from the Falklands war."

There was a short pause. "Ken?"

"Sorry. An important email just pinged in. You want me to ask about a former member of three para?"

"Yes."

"Why am I asking the paras this?"

"If Terry Creighton has no such history of these problems, he might just be the last man to see William Grant alive."

There was another short pause. "Okay Kelly. I'll text you what I find out." The call went dead.

Kelly got up from the bed and went back to the window. She looked up at the bright blue sky, closed her eyes and soaked up the early morning sunshine streaming through the window and onto her face.

8:30am Saturday 16th May

Crosby sat in his chair at the breakfast table with his shoulders slumped forward over the table. He looked up from stirring his mug of coffee and through bloodshot eyes, he saw Kelly walking towards him. He let out a low groan and put the teaspoon down on the table next to the cup. He took a sip of the steaming coffee and cradled the mug in both hands. He did not take his eyes off Kelly as she got closer. She was wearing black, skintight jeans, tucked into calf length boots and a light blue cotton shirt. As always, her short red hair was immaculately styled, and her makeup was understated.

Crosby forced a smile. "Good morning."

From a few feet away, Kelly had seen Crosby's bloodshot eyes and knew that something was wrong. She pulled out a chair and sat down across the table from him. "You look like shit. What's happened?"

Crosby ignored the question and took another sip of coffee.

The landlady, Maggie, appeared at the table. She ignored Crosby. "Good morning Kelly. What would you like for breakfast?"

Kelly shot a concerned look at Crosby and then back at the landlady.

Maggie shook her head very slightly.

Kelly forced a smile. "Strong black coffee and a soft boiled egg with toast, please."

The landlady nodded, lightly placed her hand on Kelly's shoulder and left the table.

Kelly sat staring at Crosby, who was still sat slumped forward and staring at the mug of coffee cradled in his hands.

After a couple of minutes of silence and no movement, Crosby took a sip of his coffee. He put the mug down on the table and forced a smile. "I'm taking the day off. I was thinking about visiting Warkworth Castle this morning and Amble this afternoon. I need all the distraction I can get right now. Would you like to come?"

Before Kelly could answer, the landlady returned to the table with her breakfast. She put the boiled egg and toast down in front of Kelly and a full English breakfast down in front of Crosby.

Crosby looked up. "I'm not hungry."

The landlady put her hands on her hips. "Eat it, it'll do you good," she ordered.

Crosby picked up the knife and fork in front of him, cut into a sausage and put it into his mouth. He chewed slowly.

Kelly leaned back in her chair, looked up and smiled her thanks to the landlady.

The landlady sighed and nodded towards Crosby.

Kelly shook her head, picked up her coffee cup and took a sip.

The landlady sighed again and retreated from the table.

Kelly put the cup down. From the look of Crosby, she thought that he should not be on his own right now. "Yes, I'd like to spend the day with you. I've never been to a castle."

Crosby nodded and forced a smile. "Not even the Tower of London or Windsor Castle?"

Kelly shook her head. "No. Never been."

Crosby pushed the plate of food away, picked up his mug and took a drink of coffee.

Warkworth Castle – 10:30am Saturday 16th May

Crosby stopped walking just outside of the entrance to the castle and pressed two on speed dial. He smiled at Kelly and turned his back on her.

The call was answered on the first ring. "Joe, are you okay?"

I'm fine Sally. Will you do me favour?"

"Yes. Of Course."

"Thanks. Contact James Marlow at Marlow Homes, and tell him that he can have the market garden and all of the land if he makes a serious offer. His card is by the telephone on the kitchen worktop."

Sally was shocked that her brother wanted to sell the market garden and its land. "Please, Joe, think about......"

Crosby cut her off. "Marlow's been after the land for ages."

Sally tried again. "Joe...."

Crosby kicked at a stone and cut her off again. "Sally, listen to me. Me and Caitlin are finished. When the debts are paid off from the sale of the land, Caitlin is to get what's left. Will you take care of that for me?"

Tears were rolling down Sally's cheeks. "Yes" she said quietly.

There was a long minute's silence, which Crosby

broke. "Sally?"

She sniffed and dabbed at her eyes with a tissue "Yes."

"I'm not coming back. I'm staying up here in Northumberland."

On the other end of the call, Crosby could hear his sister sobbing. His heart grew heavy and silent tears rolled down his cheeks. He ended the call and wiped the tears away with the back of his hand.

From only a few feet away, Kelly heard the conversation. She felt sorry for Crosby and wondered if he would ever find the happiness, which had died with Rosie.

Crosby put his phone into his jeans pocket, turned and forced a smile. He started walking towards Kelly. "Let's go in. You'll like it, I promise."

Kelly smiled back and as Crosby reached her, she linked arms with him. She did not say a word, just gripped his arm tight and pulled him close.

Kelly took her credit card back from the woman behind the counter, said, "Thank you," and walked out of the small shop to join Crosby. He had both hands shoved deep into his jeans pockets and his shoulders were slumped forward. He looked defeated and she sighed.

Crosby turned just as Kelly reached him.

Kelly smiled, handed him the audio tour and linked arms. She quickly scanned the walls and settled her eyes on the castle keep. "I've never been to a castle. This is cool."

Crosby forced a smile, put on the headphones for the audio tour and waited for the speaking to begin.

Amble, Northumberland – 1:30pm Saturday 16th May

The Trawler pub was busy and alive with chatter from tourists and families out for a day to the Northumberland coast.

Crosby's mood had brightened since the morning, but he was still not his usual self.

Kelly looked out of the window and nodded towards it. "Your car has got some fans."

Crosby smiled, but did not look up from the menu. "So long as it still has wheels when we come to leave here."

Kelly started laughing.

Crosby still did not look up from the menu. "I think I'll have the cod and chips."

Five minutes later, Crosby was at the bar ordering food and drinks. "It's table ten. Two cod and chips, a pint of McEwan's Best Scotch and a half of cider, please."

The woman punched the order into the till and looked up smiling. "That'll be twenty eight pounds fifty, please" and she reached under the bar for the drinks glasses.

Crosby put three, ten pound notes down on the bar and waited for the drinks.

The barmaid put the drinks down on the bar,

picked up the money and turned her back on Crosby to ring the sale through the till.

Crosby picked up the drinks and walked away from the bar without collecting his change.

As Crosby sat down, Kelly asked, "So what's our next move on the case?"

Crosby took a sip of beer. "I'm having a day off."

Kelly stared at him and he sighed, the pint glass hovering just in front of his mouth. "Okay. On Monday morning we go to the police and we report that we've found William Grant, but that his brother is now missing."

Kelly took a sip of cider and put the glass down on the beer mat to her right. "We don't know for sure that William has assumed Robert's identity and is now living with Anna. How do we prove that?"

Crosby did not answer, he was looking through the window at a group of twenty somethings admiring his car.

Kelly continued, "If we have no proof, the police will think we're crackpots."

A grin spread across Crosby's face. "Probably." He took a long drink of beer and continued. "We tell them that if we're wrong, which I believe we're not, then they can charge us with wasting police time. We then turn up at Grant's home with a Copper or two in tow and ask him to give his face a good rub down with a makeup removing wipe. You said it yourself, you thought that Grant was wearing makeup."

"But it's only a hunch Joe. I'm not sure at all."

Crosby took another long drink of beer. "Learn to go with your hunches Kelly. If you play it safe, you'll never solve any cases."

Kelly nodded, smiled thinly and took sip of cider. "You think it will reveal a freckle over his right eyebrow?"

"Yes."

Kelly thought for a moment and asked. "Then what?"

Crosby ran his finger down the glass, wiping away a line of condensation. "If it is William Grant who is now living with Anna, which I believe it is, then it's case closed for us. We've found him, which is all that the firm was hired to do."

Kelly nodded. "I see. Then it's up to the police to find out what happened to Robert."

Crosby acknowledged the deduction by raising his glass and draining what was left of the beer in it.

Silence descended on the table, just as their food arrived.

Alnmouth – 8:00pm Saturday 16th May

Crosby stood with his hands in his jeans pockets, looking out over the mouth of the river Aln towards the North Sea. His feet were slowly sinking into the top of the sand dune.

Kelly lifted her chin and closed her eyes, savouring the light, warm breeze blowing off the sea. She opened her eyes and saw Crosby staring at a young couple holding hands and walking towards them across the sand dunes. She gently put her hand on his shoulder. "Joe" she said softly.

Crosby turned slightly, and she saw the single tear rolling down his cheek. "Joe. Are you okay?"

Crosby turned his face away and nodded towards the young couple who were getting closer. "Seeing them reminds me of me and Rosie and brings back some very happy memories."

Kelly turned her attention back to the young couple. They had stopped and were now in each other's arms, kissing.

Crosby sniffed, and another tear rolled down his cheek. "Right where they are now, is where I proposed to Rosie."

Kelly's jaw dropped. She had not known that Crosby and Rosie had been engaged to be married and she turned to Crosby. She was about to speak but

Crosby continued. "She said yes. It was only five days before she was killed. I didn't get the chance to buy her an engagement ring, I wanted her to choose the one she fell in love with."

Kelly felt like her heart was crying out in pain for Crosby and tears started to flow down her face. She fumbled around in her bag for a tissue, but there was none. "Fuck!"

Crosby ignored the profanity, his eyes were fixed on the couple, who were now laughing and chasing after each other, just like he and Rosie had done.

Kelly wiped her tears away with the sleeve of her jacket and said softly, "I'm so sorry Joe."

Crosby did not hear Kelly's kind words, he was deep in a daydream, watching himself and Rosie play on the sand and then lose themselves in their kisses.

Fifteen minutes later as they were walking back to the Fisherman's Rest, Kelly asked, "What will you do when the case is over?"

Crosby stopped and kicked at some gravel on the pavement. He shoved his hands into his jeans pockets. "The market garden is being sold, so I'll be homeless." He started walking again.

After a couple of minutes of walking in silence, Kelly asked, "Where will you go?"

"You really are a nosey bitch, aren't you Kelly?"

"Yes. Answer the question."

Crosby sighed. "I'm staying up here. Another new start. I suppose you'll go back to Brightside?"

Kelly nodded. "I suppose I will."

The Fisherman's Rest, Alnmouth - 9:30pm Saturday 16th May

Crosby laid back on the bed and pressed four on speed dial. The call was answered on the second ring. "Andrew, it's Joe. Are you at the farm?"

"Hi Joe. It's been a while and yes, I'm at the farm."

"Are you free for me to pay you a visit tomorrow morning?"

"Sure."

"Thanks. I'll see you tomorrow" and Crosby ended the call.

Crosby reached over and put the phone on the bedside table. He clasped his hands behind his head, closed his eyes and began to dream of happy times spent on the beach with Rosie.

Waterloo Bridge, London – 2:00am Sunday 17th May

Caitlin walked slowly across the bridge towards the south bank of the river. Half way across she stopped, drained what was left of the bottle of vodka and looked across the river towards the City of London. She looked up and down the bridge, saw that she was alone and threw the empty bottle into the river. Caitlin climbed onto the side of the bridge and without any hesitation, she jumped into the black, fast flowing river. She allowed the strong undercurrent to pull her down and away from the bridge.

9:30am Sunday 17th May

Kelly looked up and smiled as the landlady put her breakfast of a soft, boiled egg and toast down in front of her. "Have you seen Joe? He didn't answer when I knocked on his room door. He had a tough day yesterday and I'm......"

The landlady put her hand lightly on Kelly's shoulder and smiled back. "Don't worry pet. He's gone to see an old friend down in Barnard Castle. He'll be back later today."

Kelly let out a sigh of relief. She nodded and smiled her thanks, and the landlady left the table.

Kelly picked up the teaspoon from the plate, took the top off the egg, dipped the end of a piece of toast into the yolk and took a bite.

She had the whole day to herself; after a couple of minutes' thought, she decided that she would take a taxi to Alnwick Castle and gardens and spend the day there.

She took another bite of toast and her phone buzzed on the table as she chewed. She picked it up and read the text from Ken Williams.

Home Farm, Barnard Castle, County Durham – 9:35am Sunday 17th May

The TR4 sped through the farmyard gates and skidded to a halt on the cobbles in front of the old farmhouse.

As Crosby got out of the car, the farmhouse door opened.

Andrew Blowers pushed his hands into his jeans pockets, leaned on the doorframe and shouted across the farmyard, "NICE CAR, JOE."

Crosby slammed the driver's door shut and grinned at his friend.

As he walked towards the farmhouse, Crosby's phone buzzed in his jeans pocket. He dug it out and read the text.

Paras have no record of Creighton psycho probs or seeing things. Kelly X.

Crosby nodded to himself and put the phone back into his jeans pocket.

Blowers held out his right hand for a handshake. "Joe, it's good to see you. Come in, Mrs. Pitt has the kettle on."

As Crosby stepped into the kitchen, the old housekeeper quickly shuffled towards him and gave him a hug. She stepped back and quickly looked him up and down. "You've lost weight Joe. I have a nice fruit loaf in the pantry which will do you a bit of good."

Crosby looked at his watch. "It's a bit early in the morning for cake, don't you think?"

The old housekeeper put her hands on her hips. "It's never too early or late for a nice slice of home baked cake."

Blowers started laughing and Mrs. Pitt shuffled off to fetch the cake from the pantry.

Blowers and Crosby sat down at the old kitchen table. "How's your gorgeous wife, Andrew?"

Blowers grinned, everyone he knew said she was gorgeous and too good for him. "Robyn's good. She's pregnant."

A smile spread across Crosby's face. He stood up and reached across the table to shake Blowers' hand. "Wow. That's great news. Congratulations mate."

Blowers shook the offered hand. "Thanks. She's due in six weeks."

Crosby was still smiling as he sat down. "Will the baby be born here, in England?"

Blowers shook his head. "No, in New York. Robyn's there now, preparing for another exhibition for the children's home she helps. I'm flying out at the end of the week and we'll come home after the baby's born."

Crosby was nodding and grinning. He was very happy for his friend. "A boy, girl or surprise?"

Blowers smiled. "Surprise. Robyn didn't want to know the baby's sex."

There was a long minute's silence, which Blowers broke. "You didn't come here just to catch up,

Joe. What's going on?"

Crosby shook his head. "No. I need your help."

Blowers nodded. "You back in the finding game?"

"Yes. It's a one off case."

"Okay. If I can help, I will."

"Do you remember a guy called Terry Creighton from your time in the paras?"

Blowers did not like talking about his time in the parachute regiment and a knot began to tighten in his stomach. "Joe. You know I don't like talking about that stuff."

Crosby nodded. "I know, but I need your help and I wouldn't ask if it wasn't important."

Blowers sighed and thought for a moment. "Yes. I think he was a sergeant in Support Company. I'll just check." He dug his phone out of his jeans pocket and pressed one on speed dial.

The call was answered on the second ring. "Hello Andrew."

"Tommy. Do you remember Terry Creighton? He was a sergeant in Support Company, wasn't he?"

There was a pause.

"Tommy?"

"Yes. Why do you want to know?"

"Just checking. Thanks Tommy," and Blowers ended the call. He put the phone down on the table just as the old housekeeper arrived at the kitchen table, holding a tray with a teapot, two mugs, a bowl of sugar, a jug of milk and two plates with a slice of fruit loaf on each.

Blowers smiled. "Thank you, Mrs. Pitt."

The old lady put her hand on Blowers' shoulder.

"You're welcome my dear," and she shuffled back to the sink full of breakfast dishes to wash.

While Blowers was reaching for a mug and the teapot, he said, "Terry Creighton was a sergeant in Support Company."

Crosby asked, "Was he discharged out of the regiment after the Falklands, because of psychological problems?"

Blowers shook his head. "No. The Terry Creighton I knew was invalided out of the regiment. Shortly after we got back from the Falklands, he was knocked off his motorbike by a drunk driver. A hit and run. He suffered serious leg, hip and back injuries. When he recovered, he was medically discharged as unfit for duty."

Crosby nodded. "Thanks, Andrew" and he took a big bite of cake. "Hmmm, this is nice cake."

Blowers grinned. "You won't find a nicer piece of fruit cake anywhere north of Scotch Corner."

At the sink and up to her elbows in hot soapy water, Mrs. Pitt heard the compliment about her cake and smiled to herself.

Alnwick Police Station - 10:00am Monday 18th May

The interview room was freezing cold. The air con was blowing straight down onto the back of Crosby's neck and he shivered. He tucked his hands under his armpits to keep them warm and glanced to his left at Kelly, who was on her phone, scrolling through her social media.

The interview room door swung open hard, startling Crosby and Kelly. They both stood up quickly behind the table as a tall, rugged faced policeman in a dark, slim fitting suit walked into the room. He did not close the door behind him.

Crosby smiled and held out his right hand for a handshake. "Joe Crosby and this is my colleague, Kelly Mathers. We're from Brightside Investigations in London."

The policeman put his hands into his suit trouser pockets, looked at his feet and shook his head. Just loud enough for Crosby and Kelly to hear, he said, "Private dicks from the smoke. Great. Just what I needed on a shitty Monday morning."

Crosby withdrew his hand and shook his head. "No. We're finders. We specialize in finding missing people," he said with more than a hint of irritation in his voice.

The policeman sighed loudly and looked up

from studying his highly polished brogue shoes. "Who's missing Mr. Crosby, or is it, who have you found who was missing?"

Crosby was just about to answer, when a man with short, blonde hair and a neatly trimmed goatee beard walked into the room. He closed the door behind him and leaned against the wall by the door. He did not introduce himself.

Crosby stared at the new arrival. "Who are you?"

The tall policeman answered. "My bag man, DS Rob Harley."

Crosby smiled. "So, that makes you a Detective Inspector."

The tall policeman showed a hint of a smile. "Good deduction. DI Jim Mills." He still had his hands in his pockets and did not offer a handshake.

Crosby's irritation was growing. "Good. Now we all know each other and can move on," he said curtly.

DS Harley pushed himself away from the wall and took two steps into the room. He nodded at Kelly. "I don't. Who are you?"

Kelly moved around the table and walked towards the Detective Sergeant. She looked him up and down as she walked, clean black oxford shoes, slim fitting light grey suit, white shirt with a small collar and a skinny dark blue tie held in place by a silver tie pin. She liked what she saw and smiled as she held out her hand for a handshake. She nodded over her shoulder towards Crosby. "I'm his bag man, Kelly Mathers."

Harley instantly liked the confident redhead and

smiled. He firmly shook the offered hand.

Kelly liked men with strong hands and her hand lingered in the policeman's.

Mills sighed loudly and raised his voice. "I'll ask again. Who have you found?"

Kelly quickly withdrew her hand from Harley's and stayed where she was.

Crosby answered. "William Grant, son of Lord and Lady Grant."

Mills stared blankly at Crosby. "Good for you and why does that warrant the involvement of Northumbria Police?"

Crosby glared at Mills and clenched his hands into fists.

Kelly saw the temper rising in Crosby and immediately broke the tension. "Because we think that William may have murdered his identical twin brother, Robert, has assumed his identity and is living with his brother's wife."

Mills turned to Kelly. His face was deadpan. "Is that so?"

"Yes."

Harley stepped towards the door and opened it. He nodded towards the corridor. "Boss, can we speak outside?"

Mills left the room without speaking another word and Harley followed, closing the door behind him.

Crosby looked at Kelly, shrugged and sat down.

Kelly let out a long, silent exhale of breath and returned to her seat next to Crosby.

Crosby put his hands under his armpits again and muttered, "I hate this room. It's bloody freezing."

Kelly turned to him. "Maybe it's this cold to make suspects feel uncomfortable during an interview under caution."

Crosby ignored the comment and just shivered, his mood becoming blacker.

Outside of the interview room, Harley looked his DI in the eye and shook his head. "This is crackers, boss. A brother killing his identical twin to assume his identity and live with his wife. That's a wild accusation."

Mills grinned. "Have you forgotten? We specialise in crackers, Rob. Besides, we need a case and a result to get the Chief Super off our backs after the Gary Passmoor fiasco."

Harley sighed and shifted his weight from his right leg to his left. He put his hands into his suit trouser pockets and sighed again. "Okay boss, but I don't think the Chief Super's going to okay the time and resources based on such a wild accusation."

Mills grinned. "I'm not going to tell her until I know for sure that we have a case."

Harley shook his head. "You're playing with fire boss."

Mills just grinned and reached for the interview room door handle.

The policemen re-entered the room and sat down opposite Crosby and Kelly. Mills drummed his fingers on the table as he looked from Crosby to Kelly and back again. "Okay. We're interested. Tell us what you know."

For the next twenty minutes, Crosby and Kelly told the policemen all about the case; that the Grant twins regularly swapped identities, that Anna and

William were expected by the family to marry, but it was Robert who proposed and married her.

The policemen looked at each other and Mills asked, "So, you think Anna thought it was William who proposed?"

Crosby shook his head. "No. It was Robert who proposed to Anna."

Mills could feel a headache starting and he massaged his temples. "So, Anna knew it was Robert who had proposed?"

Kelly nodded. "Yes."

Harley continued the questions. "If they're identical twins, how do you know it's William who is now living with Anna?"

Kelly answered. "We don't for sure, but if you ask him to wipe his face thoroughly with a make-up removing wipe.........."

Mills leaned back in his chair and started laughing, and Harley shook his head, muttering, "This is bloody crackers, man."

Kelly patiently waited for Mills to stop laughing and when he did, she continued. "Look. William has a freckle above his right eyebrow and Robert has a freckle above his left. I'm positive that the Robert Grant I supposedly saw was wearing make-up to hide his real freckle and that he is in fact, William Grant."

Crosby cut in. "And that begs the question, where is Robert Grant?"

Mills looked at his sergeant, who just shrugged and said, "I told you this is crackers, boss."

Mills turned back to Crosby. "He could have just left Anna."

Crosby shook his head. "No. We have a witness

194

who will say that he saw the brothers out in the dead of the night on the coastal path behind the Grants' house, and that they argued and fought."

Mills leaned forward, resting his elbows on the table. "So, we show up at the Grants' house with a pack of make-up wipes, ask him to wipe his face and start a murder enquiry?"

Crosby grinned. "If you put it like that Detective Inspector, yes."

Harley let out a short laugh. "Like you said boss, we specialise in crackers."

A grin spread across Mills' face. "That we do Rob, that we do."

Howick - 4:00pm Monday 18th May

DI Jim Mills knocked on the old, wooden front door, stepped back and waited for it to open. He smiled as a beautiful woman with pale skin, light ginger hair and green eyes opened the door and stood before him.

"Can I help you?" she asked.

Mills was still smiling. "Anna Grant?"

"Yes."

Mills flashed his warrant card. "Northumbria police. I'm DI Mills and this is DS Harley. Is your husband home?"

Harley smiled and flashed his warrant card.

Anna Grant looked past the two policemen and the police squad car with a male and female police officer standing by it, to Crosby and Kelly standing by the red TR4.

Mills brought her attention back to him. "Mrs. Grant. Is your husband home?"

She studied Mills' rugged features for a moment and said quietly, "Yes."

Mills smiled. Then may we come in to speak to him?"

Anna Grant held the door open wide and stepped aside.

Seeing the policemen step forward to enter the house, Crosby and Kelly left the TR4 and quickly followed them into the house, before Anna Grant could close the door on them. As they passed her in the doorway, Crosby nodded and Kelly smiled thinly.

Anna Grant slammed the door shut, squeezed past Crosby, Kelly and the policemen and went into the study saying, "Darling, the police are here to see you."

Grant looked up from his laptop and slammed the lid down. "WHAT NOW!"

Mills entered the room with Harley following immediately behind. He smiled and flashed his warrant card. "I'm DI Mills and this is DS Harley, Northumbria police."

Grant remained seated in his chair and noticed Crosby and Kelly standing in the doorway and ignored Mills. He pointed at Crosby and Kelly and shouted, "WHAT ARE THOSE TWO DOING HERE?"

Mills ignored the outburst. "We're here about your brother, Mr. Grant."

Grant turned to the policeman and snapped "What about him?"

Mills smiled. "Harley!"

The Detective Sergeant stepped forward and held out a make-up removing wipe. "Please wipe your face Mr. Grant."

Grant stared in disbelief at the wipe. "What's that?"

Anna Grant answered. "It's a make-up removing wipe, darling."

Mills pushed his hands into his suit trouser pockets. "Indulge us, please, Mr. Grant. Please take the wipe from DS Harley and thoroughly wipe your face."

Grant stood up and shook his head. "No. This is preposterous."

Harley still held the wipe towards Grant. "Why not Mr. Grant? It's only a make-up wipe, it won't bite you."

Grant looked at Anna, but she was looking at the floor to avoid eye contact with him. He glared at Harley. "I'm not wiping my face with that."

Mills took a step towards Grant, his tall frame looming over him. His face was deadpan. "Well, Mr. Grant, we'll do this at the station, shall we?"

Grant's face started to turn red and his nostrils flared. He snatched the wipe from Harley and angrily stared to wipe his face.

A few seconds later, Grant puffed out his chest, glared at Mills and threw the used make-up wipe at him. "There. Are you happy now?"

Mills let the used make-up wipe bounce off him and fall onto the carpet. He smiled, because what had looked like a small freckle above Grant's left eye, had now disappeared. He pointed to a spot just above Grant's right eyebrow. "You've missed a bit."

Grant shook his head. "No, I haven't."

Mills was still smiling. You have missed a spot and if you don't wipe that area of your face, DI Harley will hold you down while I wipe your face."

Harley grinned as he held out a fresh make-up wipe.

Grant's shoulders slumped, and he sighed loudly. He was defeated. He meekly took the make-up wipe from Harley and wiped above his right eyebrow. A small freckle appeared. He dropped the wipe and looked at Anna, who had her hand over her mouth and tears rolling down her cheeks.

DS Harley stepped closer to Grant and Mills

said, sarcastically, "Hello Mr. William Grant, nice to meet you."

Grant tried to bluster his way out of the situation one more time and shouted, "NO. I'M NOT! MY NAME IS ROBERT GRANT, PROVE I'M NOT HIM!"

Mills was calm. "Your brother, Robert, has a small freckle over his left eyebrow and yours has just been wiped off. You now have a freckle over your right eyebrow and that makes you William Grant."

Defeat hit Grant like a hammer and he slumped into the chair and looked at his feet. He sighed loudly.

Mills continued. "As I said, we're here about your brother. Please come with us to the station to answer some questions."

Harley stepped closer to Grant. "Mr. Grant."

William Grant looked up at Anna, but she turned away from him, wiping her tears away with a tissue.

Mills turned to Anna. "You too, Mrs. Grant. There are some questions I need you to answer."

Crosby smiled to himself, nudged Kelly and whispered in her ear, "Our case is now closed."

Crosby and Kelly watched the uniformed police officers open the rear doors of the squad car and Anna and William Grant get into the car.

A smile spread across Crosby's face as Rosie whispered into his ear, "Well done Joe."

The Fisherman's Rest, Alnmouth – 5:00pm Monday 18th May

As Kelly followed Crosby through the door into the bar, her phone rang in her bag. She dug it out, saw that the call was from the Investigations Director, Ken Williams, and pressed 'Answer' on the screen. "Hello Ken."

There was a pause, "Kelly, I have some bad news."

"What is it Ken?"

"Bill Pike is dead. His body washed up in the Thames this morning. I'm at the morgue now and have just identified his body. The police think he was murdered, stabbed in the neck and pushed into the river to drown."

Kelly had stopped walking and as Crosby turned around to ask her what she wanted to drink, he saw her knees buckle and put her hand on a table to steady herself. He took a couple of steps towards her. "Kelly what's the matter."

Tears were streaming down Kelly's cheeks and she managed to say, "Bill Pike's been murdered."

Crosby felt nothing and is face was deadpan as he muttered very quietly under his breath "Good riddance."

Kelly was a shaking wreck and Crosby stepped

up to her. He pressed 'End' on the phone screen and put his arm around her. Crosby moved Kelly towards the bar saying, "Let's get a good stiff drink inside you."

Alnwick Police Station - 6:00pm Monday 18th May

DI Jim Mills entered interview room one and left the door open. He paused, put his hands into his suit trouser pockets and watched Anna Grant pick at her fingernails.

Outside in the corridor and out of the sight of Anna Grant, DS Rob Harley leaned a shoulder against the wall by the door.

Anna Grant looked up, suddenly aware that she was being watched.

Mills smiled, walked over to the table and sat down opposite her. He put a disk into the recorder and pressed record. "DI Mills interviewing Mrs. Anna Grant at eighteen oh two hours on eighteenth of May twenty fifteen." He leaned back in his chair. "Mrs. Grant, I want to make it clear that you are not under arrest, but that you are helping us with our enquiries."

She nodded, and silent tears started to flow down her cheeks.

Mills ignored the tears and nodded at the recorder. "For the record please."

"I understand," she said quietly.

Mills continued. "You are free to leave at any time. Do you understand Mrs. Grant?"

She nodded again and in the same quiet voice said, "I understand." Her tears kept on flowing.

Mills clasped his hands behind his head. "Good. Did you know that William was going to turn up at your house?"

Anna sniffed and wiped her tears away with a tissue she had retrieved from the cuff of her sleeve. "Yes. We had been in contact for a few weeks and had arranged it."

Mills nodded. "I see. Tell me what you had planned."

She took a deep breath and quietly said, "Okay." She sniffed and dabbed under her nose with the tissue. "William was to turn up at the house, remind Robert that he had gained my hand in marriage by deception, and that he would expose that to his parents if he did not leave."

"So you thought that you were marrying William?"

"Yes."

Mills leaned forward, resting his elbows on the table. "Why would telling Lord and Lady Grant that Robert had deceived you, bother him?"

Anna smiled thinly. Robert and William may be twins, but they are very different people. William does not care what his parents think, but Robert....." She tailed off into her own private thoughts.

Mills waited a long few seconds. "Mrs. Grant?"

Anna came back to the present. She sniffed and again dabbed at her nose with the tissue. "William knew that by turning up at the house unannounced, Robert would be worried about what he was up to, so he lured him outside in the early hours. William said that they argued and that he had hit Robert with his torch. He said that he left Robert lying on the coast path behind the house."

Mills said nothing and waited for Anna to fill the uncomfortable silence.

She leaned forward in her chair and glared at him with defiance in her eyes. With some venom in her tone she said, "Robert was alive when William left him."

Mills nodded. "William told you all this?"

"Yes."

"And you believe him?"

"Yes, I do," she said forcefully.

Mills smiled slightly. "When did William assume Robert's identity?"

"Right after he left Robert on the coast path and got into bed with me."

Mills leaned back in his chair and clasped his hands behind his head. "Where is Robert now?"

Anna shook her head. "I don't know. He left that night and I've not heard from him since."

"So, the plan was to get Robert to leave, for William to assume Robert's identity and for you both to live happily ever after?"

Anna nodded. "Yes. William would only have to pretend to be Robert in public."

"And in the presence of Lord and Lady Grant."

Anna ignored the comment.

Mills continued. "If William only wore makeup in public, why was he wearing it when we turned up at your house?"

"He had a business meeting earlier and must have forgotten to remove it."

Mills nodded. "I see."

Silence descended upon the interview room.

Mills waited for Anna to speak and divulge some more information, but she did not, she just glared at him from across the table.

Mills leaned forward on his elbows on the table. "How do you know that William did not dump Robert over the cliff while he was dazed?"

Anna shook her head "No. William would not do that. He would not kill his own brother." Tears began flowing down her cheeks again and she wiped them away with the tissue.

Mills smiled. "Thank you for your cooperation Mrs. Grant. You are free to leave. WPC Hjort is just outside the door and she will drive you home." He stopped the recorder, stood up scraping his chair backwards and left the room with the door wide open.

On hearing "You are free to leave," DS Harley left his post by the door of interview room one and entered interview room two next door. He left the door open and took up a position against the wall to the right of William Grant.

Grant did not speak, he just glared at him.

A grin spread across Harley's face.

DI Mills entered the interview room and slammed the door closed behind him. He put his hands into his suit trouser pockets and stared at William Grant for a long few seconds.

Grant looked up from behind the table and glared defiantly back at him.

A thin smile spread across Mills' face and he nodded to DS Harley, who pushed himself away from the wall to Grant's right, walked over to the table and put a disk into the recorder. He pressed the record button and went back to his position against the wall.

Mills said loudly, "DI Mills and DS Harley interviewing Mr. William Grant at eighteen fifteen hours on eighteenth of May twenty fifteen."

Grant still glared at him.

Mills leaned against the wall by the door and his smile disappeared. "You left Robert alive on the coastal path behind his house?"

Grant still glared at him, "Yes."

Did you plan to physically hurt your brother?"

"No."

"Did you go straight back to the house?"

Grant shook his head. "No. I walked along the coastal path for a while, thinking about what I had just done. I mean, I had just hit my brother with the torch."

Harley spoke, "And?"

Grant sighed. "An hour later I returned to the spot where I had left Robert, but he was gone. I searched around the outside of the house and inside for him, but I could not find him."

Mills cut in, "And you assumed Robert's identity when you got into bed with Anna?"

"Yes."

"Was that planned between you and Anna?"

Grant stared blankly at Mills.

Mills raised his voice a little, "Mr. Grant, did you and Anna plan for you to assume Robert's identity that night?"

Grant leaned back in in his chair and smiled thinly. "No."

Mills pushed himself away from the wall. "Well, Mr. Grant. There's now a little problem. You see, Anna says that you and her planned for you to assume Robert's identity as soon as he had left, which was that night."

Grant shook his head and still smiled. "No. I only decided to become Robert when I found his note on the kitchen table early the next morning."

Mills and Harley exchanged glances. Harley spoke, "Do you have the note?"

Grant smiled. He took his wallet out of his trouser pocket, opened it and pulled out a folded piece of paper. He held it out for Mills to take from him.

Mills took the paper, unfolded it and read aloud *"I'm leaving. You can have Anna."* He handed the note to Harley.

Harley read the note and put it down on the table in front of Grant.

Mills continued the questioning, "So, Robert left. As easy as that?"

Grant's smile grew into a grin. "Yes. I won. I got the girl."

Mills leaned back against the wall. "It's strange that Robert left without packing a suitcase. Don't you think?"

The grin disappeared as Grant looked Mills dead in the eye. "I don't know if Robert did or did not pack a suitcase. Who knows what was going through his head at the time. Maybe he had a breakdown and left with nothing but the clothes on his back."

Mills glanced at Harley, who took up the questioning, "When did you tell Anna who you really were?"

"About a week later."

"So, she thought that you were Robert the next morning?"

"Yes. I got up early, had a shower, got dressed

into some of Robert's clothes and covered the freckle over my right eyebrow with some of Anna's makeup I found in the bathroom."

Mills reached over and opened the door. "Anna wasn't upset that it took you a week to tell her who you really were?"

The grin reappeared as Grant shook his head "No. She said that she knew I wasn't Robert, because of the way I made love to her."

Mills pushed himself away from the wall. "We'll keep a hold of the note and I'll need you to provide a sample of your hand writing to Sergeant Green, who's standing right outside this door. Then you're free to leave."

Harley pushed himself away from the wall, walked over to the table and stopped the recording. He then picked up the note and followed Mills out of the door.

Sergeant Green nodded to Harley as he stepped out into the corridor and then entered the room holding a sheet of paper and a pen.

From Mills' office window on the second floor, Mills and Harley watched William Grant leave the police station.

Harley shook his head. "Boss, that's the biggest load of bull shit I've heard from those two. And they couldn't even get their story straight about William assuming Robert's identity."

Mills grunted and looked at his bag man. "Get the two sets of handwriting analysed urgently. I want to know if William wrote the supposed note from Robert. I'll speak to the Chief Super about getting a warrant and some uniforms to search the Grants' house, grounds, along the coastal path and the surrounding area."

Harley nodded. "Yes boss" and he turned and left the office.

Mills shouted after him. "We'll start the search at seven tomorrow morning."

Harley did not stop walking, he just waved his hand in acknowledgement.

7:30pm Monday 18ᵗʰ May

DI Mills knocked twice on the open door and waited to be invited into the office.

Chief Superintendent Julie Wilkes turned the page of the report on the desk in front of her and scowled. "COME," she barked.

Mills stepped into the office and sat down in the chair the other side of the desk.

The Chief Super looked up. "Make yourself at home why don't you, Jim."

Mills grinned.

She continued. "The station rumour mill says you've got yourself a murder case. One of Lord and Lady Grant's twins I believe."

Mills pulled a face. "Not quite, boss. We have a missing husband, Robert Grant, and his twin brother William has assumed his identity. I need a warrant and some uniforms to search Robert's house and surrounding area tomorrow morning."

"How do you know the husband has just not left to make himself a new life?"

Mills shifted in his chair. "I don't."

Julie Wilkes sighed and held up the report. "Do you know what this is, Jim?"

"Pieces of paper in a nice binder."

She glared at Mills from across the desk. "Smart

arse. No. It's confirmation of the station budget, for the year and it's been cut again. We're only going to be able to afford to put the bare minimum of uniforms out of the streets and forget about any overtime work." She shook her head and dropped the report onto the desk in front of her. She sighed. "The answer's no, Jim, unless you can bring me some kind of confession, I can't give you the resources."

"Boss. I...."

She cut him off with a wave of her hand. "Sorry Jim, this conversation is finished."

Mills sighed and pushed himself up from the chair. He left the room without another word and Chief Superintendent Wilkes returned to being depressed by the content of the budget report.

Mills was on his phone as he walked back to his office. He got voicemail. "Rob. No warrant and no uniforms for a search. Budget cuts, the bastards." He ended the call, shoved the phone into the inside pocket of his jacket and swore again.

The Fisherman's Rest, Alnmouth – 9:00pm Monday 18th May

DS Rob Harley walked into the bar and quickly scanned the room. He smiled when he saw Crosby and Kelly sitting at a table to the right of the bar. He walked up to the bar and smiled as he said, "A pint of the usual please, Maggie."

The landlady smiled back. "Coming up Rob."

Kelly looked over Crosby's left shoulder and saw the landlady hand Harley his pint of beer. She smiled at Crosby. "Excuse me for a minute," and she rose from her chair and walked over to the bar, where Harley stood taking a long drink of McEwan's Best Scotch.

Crosby twisted in his chair to see where Kelly was going.

Harley put his drink down on the bar and wiped his mouth with the back of his hand.

"What are you doing here Detective Sergeant?"

Harley smiled. "This is my local. I live just around the corner on Grosvenor Terrace."

Kelly smiled back. "I thought you might be keeping tabs on us."

Harley shook his head. Nope. Just popped in for a pint after a long, shitty day."

"I see. Do you mind if I join you? Mine's a half of cider."

Harley nodded towards Crosby, who was just getting up from the table. "Won't your boss mind?"

Kelly let out a short laugh and shook her head. "No. he'll be fine."

Crosby walked over to Harley and Kelly. He nodded to the policeman, "Detective Sergeant."

"Mr. Crosby."

Crosby turned to Kelly. "I'm going out to get some fresh air."

Kelly smiled. "Okay Joe," and she gave him a hug.

Cosby stopped at the door and looked back at Kelly and Harley. He smiled as they laughed together and then stepped outside into the street.

10:30pm Monday 18th May

Crosby had been sitting on a bench, looking out over the mouth of the river Aln for over an hour. He was relaxed and at peace with himself. He watched a woman with blonde hair, tied back in a ponytail, walk over the sand dunes towards him. As she got closer a smile spread across his face.

She stopped a couple of feet away from him. "Hi Joe. It's a lovely night."

A silent tear rolled down Crosby's cheek. "Hello Rosie. Yes, it is." He closed his eyes for a moment and thought he heard her whisper in his ear, "You're going to be fine, Joe." When he opened his eyes, Rosie was gone. He smiled and nodded to himself, got up from the bench and started walking back to The Fisherman's Rest.

Alnmouth station - 10:00am Tuesday 19th May

Crosby opened the passenger side door of the TR4 and Kelly got out of the car. He got a whiff of her perfume and under his breath he said, "J'adore."

Kelly thought she heard him say something. "What?"

"Oh, nothing."

Kelly smiled and lifted her suitcase off the back seat.

There was an awkward silence between them and Crosby dug his hands deep into his jeans pockets. He looked at the ground and kicked at a small stone.

Kelly smiled at Crosby's awkwardness and gave him a hug and a kiss on the cheek. She stepped back and asked, "Are you really finished with Brightside?"

Crosby nodded "Yes. I'm staying up here. Thought I might set up a small private investigations business."

Kelly grinned. "See, Joe. I told you that you were back."

Crosby nodded and then said, "I've liked working with you. What do you think about leaving Brightside and London and coming up here to work with me. Equal partners?"

Kelly looked Crosby dead in the eyes, staring at him for a long few seconds to see if he was serious. She decided that he was. "I'll think about it Joe. I really will."

Crosby nodded. "Okay. I guess you should get going. Your train will be here in a few minutes. Oh! And tell Ken Williams I will email him my report."

Kelly nodded and smiled. "Okay." She pulled up the handle of her suitcase and walked away, dragging it behind her. "I'LL BE SEEING YOU JOE CROSBY," she shouted without looking back.

"I hope so." Crosby said quietly to himself as he was getting into the driver's seat of the TR4.

The Fisherman's Rest, Alnmouth - 1:30pm Tuesday 19th May

Crosby put a piece of gammon into his mouth and as he looked up, he saw DI Mills walking towards his table. He put the knife and fork down on his plate and chewed slowly.

The policeman stood tall over the table. "Mr. Crosby, may I sit down?"

Crosby nodded and continued chewing.

Mills noisily pulled the chair out from under the table and sat down opposite Crosby. "I'd like you to introduce me to the man who saw the Grant brothers arguing."

Crosby took a large swallow of water and asked, "How'd you know I was staying here?"

Mills grinned. "Harley told me about running into you and Miss Mathers here last night."

Crosby nodded and took another large swallow of water. "You want to talk to Terry Creighton?"

"Yes."

"Where?"

"Where he saw the brothers arguing."

"When?"

"Today."

Crosby took another drink of water and studied the policeman. "Okay. I'll go and see him this afternoon and I'll call you to confirm when and where. That's if he wants to speak to you."

Mills nodded and reached into the inside pocket of his suit jacket and pulled out a card. He put it down on the table and pushed it towards Crosby's plate.

Crosby did not look at the card. "Thanks. If there's nothing else, I'd like to finish my lunch in peace."

Mills nodded, rose from the table scraping the chair back and left.

Crosby watched the policeman leave and then picked up the fork. He stabbed two chips and put them into his mouth. The card remained on the table next to his plate.

Howick – 3:00pm 19th May

Terry Creighton looked out of the dirty window as he heard a car stop outside. He recognized Crosby instantly, got up from the old wooden chair and walked across the kitchen to the door. He opened it before Crosby could knock.

Crosby was smiling. "Hello Mr. Creighton, can I come in?"

Creighton opened the door wide without a word and Crosby stepped into the kitchen.

Creighton sat back down on the old wooden chair and studied Crosby for a moment. "What can I do for you Mr. Crosby?"

Crosby had not been invited to sit, so he stood with his hands in his jeans pockets. He explained that William Grant had taken his brother's identity and that the police were now looking into the disappearance of Robert Grant.

Creighton listened intently, never taking his eyes off Crosby. "Why are you telling me this, Mr. Crosby?"

"Would you be willing to meet with the police where you saw the brothers arguing, and tell them what you saw that night?"

Creighton looked out of the dirty window. "When?"

"Today."

"No."

"Why not?"

Creighton sighed and turned to look Crosby dead in the eyes. "Mr. Crosby, I don't want anything to with this. I just want to be left alone to try and live my life in what little peace I can find."

Crosby nodded. "I understand. But if you don't help now, the police will come here to question you, and if you still refuse, you could be charged with obstructing the police in a murder enquiry."

Creighton jumped up from the chair and there was anger in his eyes, although his voice remained calm, "The answer is still no. Now leave my home."

Crosby half held his hands up in surrender. He dug a scrap of paper and a pencil out of his jacket pocket and scribbled down his mobile number. He put the paper down on the table, turned, and walked towards the door. He stopped, turned and looked over at the fireplace. He nodded at the photograph of Creighton as a member of the parachute regiment at the end of the Falklands war. "You know, I have a friend who was in Three Para during the Falklands war."

Creighton looked at the photograph. "What's his name?"

"He's in that photograph. Andrew Blowers," and Crosby stepped outside into the bright sunshine. He stood for a moment, his eyes closed and soaking up the sunshine on his face.

Crosby was just opening the car door when Creighton appeared in the doorway.

"Why should I help the police, Mr. Crosby?"

Crosby smiled, "That's an easy one. Because it's

the right thing to do."

Creighton leaned against the door frame and pushed his hands deep into the pockets of his grubby combat trousers.

Crosby got into the TR4 and slammed the door shut. He started the car and put the gear stick into first. He looked across at Creighton and shouted above the noise of the engine, "CALL ME."

Creighton shouted back. "I'LL THINK ABOUT IT, MR. CROSBY."

Crosby released the handbrake, stamped down on the accelerator pedal and the car sped away, leaving Creighton still leaning against the door frame.

The Fisherman's Rest, Alnmouth - 4:00pm Tuesday 19th May

Crosby held Mills' card in one hand and his phone in the other. He checked that he had tapped in the correct number and tapped 'call' on the screen.

The call was answered on the second ring. "DI Mills. Northumbria Police."

"It's Joe Crosby. Terry Creighton is not keen to talk to you."

Mills threw his pen across his office. "I don't fucking care if he's keen or not. I'm speaking to him, today. Give me his address."

Crosby shook his head. "No. Storming right in there will do no good. Meet me on the lane outside of the Grants' house in Howick and I'll take you there. Let me smooth the way for you first."

Mills jumped up and sent his chair backwards into the wall. "I'm on my way," and he ended the call.

Howick - 5:00pm Tuesday 19th May

Crosby banged hard on the old cottage door. "TERRY! IT'S JOE CROSBY AND DI MILLS OF NORTHUMBRIA POLICE."

There was no answer.

Mills stooped and looked through the dirty window into the cottage. "It looks empty."

Crosby banged on the door again.

"He's gone," a voice said from over Crosby's shoulder.

Crosby spun around, and Mills stood up from peering through the window, to see an old man in dirty overalls and a flat cap stood two feet away from them.

Mills dug out his warrant card and flashed it. "DI Mills, Northumbria police. Who are you?"

"Tom Brown. I own the cottage." The old man dug a dirty rag out of a pocket and began wiping his hands on it. He nodded towards Crosby. "I heard Terry shout who you are." He continued to wipe his hands. "Terry's gone. Left with his bags about half an hour ago."

Mills put his warrant card back into the inside pocket of his suit jacket. "Did he say where he was going?"

The old man shook his head. "No. He mumbled something about Robert Grant from the old rectory being murdered and that he wasn't going to stick around for it to be pinned on him."

Crosby asked, "Which way did he go?"

The man half turned and pointed. "Across the fields."

Crosby looked at Mills. "It looks like he's done a runner."

Mills shook his head. "Fuck!"

Crosby turned to the old man. "Thank you Mr. Brown,"

The old man nodded, turned and walked away.

5:20pm Tuesday 19th May

Mills stood by his car near to the Grants' house and dug his phone out of the inside pocket of his suit jacket. He pressed two on speed dial and paced up and down, while he was waiting for the call to be answered.

A minute later, DS Harley answered. "Sorry boss. I'm driving and had to find somewhere to pull over."

Mills grunted. "Start looking through Robert Grant's bank accounts. See if there has been any withdrawals from his account since he's been missing."

"First thing in the morning, boss."

Mills stopped pacing. "No. Tonight, Rob."

"I have plans for tonight, boss."

"Cancel them." Mills ended the call. He put the phone back into the jacket pocket and groaned as a headache started to come. He banged his fist down on the roof of the car and swore. He opened the driver's door, got into the car, slammed the door shut and started the engine. He sat for a moment and dug his phone out of his jacket pocket. He pressed one on speed dial and waited.

The call was answered on the fourth ring. "Hello pet."

Mills smiled. "Hello. Get your glad rags on, we're going out for dinner tonight. It's been a shit day and I could do with a few drinks and some good company. I'll be there in thirty minutes to pick you up."

"This is a surprise. Is everything okay?"

"Yes. Just be ready."

"Okay. See you soon," and the call ended.

Mills tossed his phone onto the front passenger seat, fastened the seat belt, put the car into drive and drove away from the grass verge.

The Fisherman's Rest, Alnmouth - 7:30pm Tuesday 19th May

Crosby smiled as the waitress put a bowl of steaming hot vegetable soup down in front of him. When she had left the table, he picked up his phone and pressed two on speed dial. The call was answered on the second ring. "Hello Sal."

"Joe. Are you okay?"

"Yes. I'm fine. Has Marlow made an offer?"

"Yes. Five hundred thousand. I think it's a bit low."

"Tell him it's a deal. Contact James Roberts Solicitors tomorrow morning, speak to James himself and put completion of the sale in motion."

"Are you sure about this, Joe?"

"Yes."

Sally sighed. "Okay."

There was a long pause which Crosby broke, suddenly realizing that he should ask, "Are you okay?"

Sally ignored the question, "Joe, Caitlin's still missing."

Crosby tried again, "Sal, are you okay?".

"Yes. Joe, did you hear what I said? Caitlin's…."

Crosby cut her off, "Tell James who is owed money and how much. It's all written down in my accounts book, which is in a drawer in the kitchen. All debts are to be settled and then what's left is to be transferred into Caitlin's bank account. Her bank statements are in a grey file box in our bedroom. You can get her bank details from one of the statements."

Sally tried again, "Joe, Caitlin's....."

Crosby cut her off again. "Sal, I don't care. It's over between us and I'm staying up here. Will you contact James Roberts tomorrow?"

Sally gave in and sighed. "Yes."

"Thanks."

There was another long few seconds of silence and then Sally asked, "You're staying up in Northumberland?"

"Yes. I'm not coming back to Rotherham. Give everything in the house to charity."

Sally did not say anything, and Crosby continued, "I'm going to finally sell the house in London and I'm going to use the money to buy a place up here."

Silent tears began to roll down Sally's face. She wiped them away with the back of her hand. "I've got to go Joe. Good night" and she pressed 'end call' on the phone screen.

Crosby put the phone down on the table and sighed. He picked up a spoon and spooned soup into his mouth. It was tasty, but he had suddenly lost his appetite. He put the spoon down, picked up his phone, scraped back his chair and left the table.

8:00pm Tuesday 19ᵗʰ May

Crosby sat down on his bed. He turned and looked at his phone on the bedside table for a few seconds, picked it up and pressed four on speed dial.

Kelly Mathers answered her phone on the third ring. "Hello Joe."

"Hi. Do you know a good estate agent in London?"

"Why?"

"I want to sell my house in Fulham, fully furnished."

"Yes. I have a girlfriend who works for Newton and Abbott. I'm sure she'll be happy to help."

Crosby told Kelly the address and where to find the spare key.

Kelly wrote down the address and read it back to him.

Crosby was nodding to himself. "Yes, that's correct. Tell your friend that I want a quick sale at a fair price and that there will be a two grand bonus in it for her if she achieves that."

There was a long pause and Kelly finally asked, "So, you're definitely staying up in Northumberland?"

"Yes."

"I'm still thinking about your offer."

Crosby smiled to himself. "Good. Take your time. There's no rush."

"Okay. I'll speak to you soon, Joe." She ended the call.

Alnwick Police Station - 10:00am Wednesday 20th May

Mills looked up from his laptop screen as DS Harley sat down in the chair in front of his desk. He leaned back in his chair, clasped his hands behind his head and waited for his bag man to speak.

"Boss, two months after Robert Grant went missing, three hundred thousand pounds was transferred from his private account to an account in Zurich."

Mills leaned forward in his chair and drummed his fingers on the desk as he thought for a minute.

"From his private account, not a joint account with Anna?"

Harley nodded. "Yes, his private account."

Mills drummed his fingers again and was thinking out loud. "How would William Grant know about his brother's private bank account if Robert was dead?"

Harley stared at his DI and waited for instructions.

Mills continued. "Go and speak to the bank manager who handled the transaction and also go and see Anna Grant. Let's see if she knew if her husband had a private account. I bet that she didn't."

Harley nodded. "Okay boss." He rose from the

chair and left Mills' office.

Mills loosened his tie, leaned back in his chair and clasped his fingers behind his head. He asked himself the question, *If Anna knew nothing about her husband's private bank account, how would William have access to it if his brother was dead?* He closed his eyes and tried to come up with an answer.

11:00am Wednesday 20th May

Anna Grant's face was a picture of anger as DS Harley walked through the door of her shop. "What do you want now Sergeant?" she hissed.

Harley smiled. "Good morning Mrs. Grant. I only have one question for you. Does your husband have a private bank account in only his name?"

The colour drained from Anna's face and she shook her head. "No. Not that I know of."

"You're sure?"

Anna sat down behind the glass topped desk and regained her composure. She looked up at the policeman. "I did not know that my husband had a private bank account."

Harley nodded and smiled. "Thank you for your time Mrs. Grant." He turned and left the shop.

As the shop door closed, Anna Grant went back to reading an article about the impressionist movement of painters.

Alnwick Police Station - 11:30am Wednesday 20th May

DI Mills tapped 'call' on the phone screen.
The call was answered on the second ring. "Joe Crosby speaking."

"It's DI Mills. I'd like you to come down to the station."

"I can be there about two o'clock. What's this about?"

Mills nodded to himself. "Good" and he ended the call.

Crosby looked at his phone for a long couple of seconds and then put it into his jeans pocket. He picked up the coffee cup and took a sip of the strong, steaming black liquid and wondered what the policeman wanted to talk to him about.

Newcastle upon Tyne – 12:00pm Wednesday 20th May

The banker stood up behind his desk as DS Harley walked into his office.

Harley flashed his warrant card. "Detective Sergeant Harley, Northumbria Police. I have some questions to ask you about Robert Grant."

The banker instantly became defensive. "You need a warrant to access private banking data." He sat down in his chair and did not offer for the policemen to sit down in the chair in front of his desk.

Harley smiled and stuffed his hands into his suit trouser pockets. He waited for banker to break the silence he had created.

The banker shifted uneasily in his chair. "Mr. Grant is no longer a customer of the bank."

Harley frowned. "Please explain."

"He closed his account with us thirty minutes ago."

Harley was startled, "He was just here?"

The banker shook his head. "No. He closed his account in a video call."

Harley thought for a moment. "Did you transfer all the money to the same account in Zurich as in January 2014?"

The banker's face was deadpan. "Yes. How do you know about that? You need a warrant….."

Harley held up his right hand and stopped the banker mid-sentence. He took his phone out of the inside pocket of his suit jacket and pressed two on speed dial for DI Mills.

The call was answered on the first ring. "Don't tell me Rob. The bank account is closed and all the money was transferred to the bank account in Zurich."

"Yes boss, just thirty minutes ago."

Mills brought his fist down hard onto his desk. "Fuck! Robert Grant is still alive, and I think William is about to disappear again."

Harley was confused, "Boss?"

Mills continued "I'll get an alert out to all the airports, ferry ports, rail stations and bus stations. You go and pick Anna Grant up and bring her to the station."

The call ended before Harley could say, "Yes boss."

Harley turned and left the banker's office without another word to him. He still had his phone in his hand.

Crosby walked into the police station and found DI Mills waiting for him in the reception area. "Follow me!" he said abruptly.

The receptionist buzzed Mills and Crosby through the door and turned her attention back to the monitor on her desk, to avoid eye contact with the grumpy DI.

Crosby followed Mills to his office without a word from him.

Mills sat down behind his desk and looked Crosby dead in the eye. "Robert Grant has cleaned out his bank account and his brother is about to disappear and join him, wherever he is."

Crosby remained standing, put his hands into his jeans pockets and shrugged. "What's that got to do with me?"

Mills leaned forward and rested on his elbows on the desk. "This has just been one big game to the Grant brothers."

Crosby started thinking and a long silence descended on the room.

Mills broke the silence. "Well? What are you thinking?"

Crosby looked the policemen dead in the eyes.

"If Robert Grant is still alive, then I think that the brothers have always been in touch with each other. Possibly a pre-planned switch of identity and clean out the bank account to start a new life somewhere sunny. Do Robert and Anna have a joint account?"

Mills leaned back in his chair and clasped his hands behind his head. "Probably."

Crosby continued. "If the joint account is cleaned out, then this could all have been about punishing Anna for stringing them along when they were younger?"

Mills sat up in his chair. "I think this whole thing goes a long way back. I think the brothers planned for Anna to marry Robert all along. As I've said, it's just a game to them."

Crosby sat down in the chair opposite Mills.

Mills continued. "I'm closing down the murder enquiry. There's no leads and no body. Robert Grant is alive, I'm sure of it."

Crosby nodded. "Okay. I still can't see what you want from me."

"Harley has just brought Anna Grant to the station. I want you behind the interview room glass to read her body language when I tell her she's been played for a fool for years by the Grant brothers."

Crosby shrugged. "Okay."

2:15pm Wednesday 20th May

Anna Grant had been alone in the interview room for thirty minutes. For the whole time, she had nervously looked around the room and had shifted in the uncomfortable plastic chair.

Mills, Harley and Crosby watched her through the glass.

Mills slapped his Sergeant on the back. "Right! She's been left to stew for long enough. Let's go and see what she knows."

Harley grinned. "Or what she doesn't know, boss."

Mills was already at the door with his hand hovering just above the door handle. He turned to his Sergeant. "That as well." He pressed down on the door handle, opened the door and left the room.

Harley followed his DI and as he reached the door he said, "Enjoy the show" without looking back at Crosby. The door swung shut behind him.

Crosby continued looking through the glass. He put his hands into his jeans pockets. His lower back was aching, and he shifted his weight from his right leg to his left to try and ease the ache.

Mills entered the interview room, closely followed by Harley. He smiled at Anna Grant as he sat across the table from her. Harley took up his usual post in interviews, leaning against the wall by the open door.

Mills was still smiling. "Did you know that your husband is still alive and that everything that has happened was pre-planned with his brother?"

Anna's right hand instantly covered her mouth and tears began to flow down her cheeks. She shook her head.

Did you know that your husband has a private bank account in Zurich?"

Anna shook her head again and the tears continued to flow.

"Did you know that earlier today, he closed his personal account in the UK and transferred all the money to the account in Zurich?

Anna shook her head, sniffed and as the tears kept flowing, she said quietly, "No."

Mills studied Anna for a moment. "Do you have online banking Mrs. Grant?"

She nodded.

Mills leaned back in his chair. "Does your husband have access to your business account?"

Anna nodded. "Yes. He's a co-director."

"I suggest you check your joint account and your business account now."

Anna dug her phone out of her bag and with shaking hands, she began tapping on the screen. Still the tears flowed down her cheeks.

After a couple of minutes, she put her phone, screen side down on the desk. She looked at Mills through watery eyes. "He's cleaned out the joint account and my business account. He's left me with nothing," and she started sobbing uncontrollably.

Mills' face softened. "I'm sorry Mrs. Grant." He stood up scraping his chair backwards. He paused looking down at the sobbing woman in front of him, turned and headed for the open door.

Harley followed Mills outside into the corridor.

Mills pushed his hands into his suite trouser pockets, shook his head and said to himself, "Poor woman."

Harley studied Mills for a few seconds as the DI studied his shoes. "What now, boss?"

Mills looked up. "Let's see what Mr. Crosby makes of Anna Grant's performance."

"Performance, boss?"

"C'mon," and Mills turned and made for the door next to the interview room.

As Mills and Harley entered the room, Crosby said, "I think she's genuine. She has no clue."

Harley chipped in. "I agree boss."

Mills nodded and turned to Harley. "Get WPC Hjort to drive Mrs. Grant home."

"Yes boss." Harley turned and left the room.

Mills turned to Crosby. "I'm shutting the whole thing down. If we pick up the Grant boys, which I doubt we will, we'll question them for the theft of money from Anna Grant's business." He held out his hand for a handshake. "Thanks for your time Mr. Crosby."

Crosby firmly shook the offered hand and watched the policeman leave the room. He turned back to the one way glass, Anna Grant was wiping her eyes with a tissue.

Brightside Investigations, Chancery Lane, London – 11:30am Monday 8th June 2015

Crosby ignored the receptionist's protests as he pushed open the large, opaque glass double doors to the open plan office. He walked purposely up the office, ignoring Kelly's smile and wave and into the second open doorway on his right.

The fat investigations manager looked up from his laptop, leaned back in the oversized soft leather chair and clasped his hands over his huge stomach. He smiled. "Have you come back to work, Joe? Good work on the Grant case, by the way."

Crosby dug into the left inside pocket of his suit jacket and pulled out a white envelope. He took a step forward and dropped the envelope onto the desk in front of the fat investigations manager. "My resignation, Ken, effective immediately. I'm done here."

As the smile disappeared from the fat investigations manager's face, Crosby turned and walked quickly out of the office. He winked and nodded at Kelly Mathers standing behind her desk and walked towards the large, opaque glass doors for the last time.

Alnwick Police Station – 12:00pm Monday 15th June 2015

While he was eating a late breakfast, Crosby had received a call from DI Jim Mills at 11:00am. All the policeman had said was that a package with Crosby's name on it had been delivered to the police station. Now he was sitting opposite Mills in his office, turning a white, A5 size envelope over in his hands.

Mills leaned back in his chair and clasped his hands behind his head. "Are you going to open it or just play with it?"

Crosby tore the top of the envelope and looked inside. He turned it upside down and a disc dropped out into his hand. He looked inside the envelope again, there was no note. He put the envelope on Mills' desk and turned the disc over in his hands, there was no label or writing on it.

Mills leaned forward in his chair and reached out across his desk towards Crosby. "Give it here, let's see what's on it."

Crosby gave the policeman the disc and walked around to his side of the desk, as he put the disc into the disc drive on his laptop.

As Crosby leaned in to look at the screen, an image of wooden decking, an expanse of still, blue water and a bright, blue sky appeared. Then the image panned to the right and revealed two men and a woman wearing a floppy, straw hat, lounging in the bright sunshine and sipping cocktails. As the image zoomed in, the lady moved off her lounger and positioned herself between the two men. They took off their dark sunglasses to reveal identical twins, William and Robert Grant and Anna Grant. Then the image was gone.

Crosby and Mills continued to stare at the blank screen for a few seconds, both trying to process what they had just watched. They turned to look at each other and at the same time said, "Fuck! She was in on it too."

Newcastle Central Station – 5:30pm Friday 21st August 2015

The train doors opened and as Crosby waited for passengers to get off, he looked left down the platform and for a flash of a moment, he thought he saw Caitlin waiting to get onto the train, and his heart skipped a beat. He forced a smile at the last person to get off the train and he stepped into the carriage. He looked left down the train and saw no sign of her. He shook his head slightly and put any thought of Caitlin out of his head as he sat down in a forward facing seat.

Amble, Northumberland – 3:30pm Friday 4th September 2015

Nelson the tabby cat stretched on the sofa and opened his only eye, as two loud knocks rang out on the apartment door.

Crosby put his book down and looked at his watch. "I'm not expecting anyone," he said to the cat. He got up from the soft leather chair, walked across the room to the door and opened it. "Jim."

DI Mills nodded. "Joe."

In the time that had elapsed since the Grant case, they had become friends. Crosby turned and walked away from the open door.

The policeman stepped through the doorway and closed the door behind him.

Crosby sat back down in the soft leather chair. "What are you doing here, Jim?"

The policeman looked around the room and nodded. "Nice digs."

"It's temporary until the old fisherman's cottage I've bought in Craster is habitable."

Mills nodded again and handed Crosby a thick buff folder. "A missing person case. A wealthy local businessman in the electronics industry who went missing eighteen months ago. The Chief Super wants you to have a crack at finding him. Dead or alive."

Crosby took the folder but did not open it. "A cold case?"

"Not quite."

Crosby dropped the folder onto the floor by his feet. "But I'm the police's last hope of finding him?"

Mills put his hands into his suit trouser pockets and smiled.

Crosby sighed. "I'll take a look at the file, see if there's anything that has been missed and follow up on any leads."

Mills nodded. "Thanks. But do it quickly and cheaply, there's only a small budget to cover limited expenses."

Crosby shook his head "So I'm probably going to end up out of pocket on this one."

Mills shrugged, turned and walked to the apartment door. "Oh! My band is playing at the Sandpiper here in Amble tonight. We start our set at eight o'clock. Come along."

Crosby smiled. "I will."

Mills nodded. "I'll put your name on the list at the door." He turned, opened the door and left, closing it behind him.

5:00pm Friday 4th September

Crosby's phone buzzed on the arm of the chair. He picked it up and tapped 'answer' on the screen. "Hi Kelly."

"Joe, I'm five minutes away, put the kettle on."

Crosby was surprised by the call and could only manage, "Ermm. Okay."

There were three knocks at the door. Crosby opened it and standing in front of him with two large suitcases either side of her, was Kelly Mathers.

"Hi Joe. I'm taking you up on your offer of a partnership."

Crosby smiled. "Great." He nodded at the suitcases. "You staying here?"

Kelly shook her head. "No. I'm moving in with Rob."

Crosby's brow furrowed "Rob?"

"DS Harley. We're engaged. A whirlwind romance" and she held out her hand with a big diamond ring on it."

Crosby stepped aside. "Congratulations."

Kelly smiled. "Thank you." She picked up the suitcases and stepped into the apartment.

Crosby closed the door. "Milk, two sugars. Right?"

Kelly flopped down into the soft leather chair and smiled. "Yes, please."

The Sandpiper, Amble – 9:30pm Friday 4th September

As Mills was introducing the last song of the night, Crosby glanced across room at the young, blonde woman for the twentieth time. She appeared to take no notice, so he turned his attention back to Mills and the band on the small stage.

Mills began to sing.

Sometimes I feel like I don't have a partner
Sometimes I feel Like my only friend
Is the city I live in…..

Crosby felt a tap on his shoulder. He turned and saw the young blonde woman standing beside him with a beaming smile. "We've been exchanging quick glances at each other all night and since you've not come over and spoken to me, I thought that I'd introduce myself to you, before the gig ends."

Crosby smiled. "I'm Joe."

She smiled back. "I'm Rose-Marie Hjort."

Crosby raised an eyebrow.

She laughed. "My dad is Swedish. In English it's Rose-Marie Hart."

Crosby smiled. "Nice to meet you Rose-Marie Hart."

"You can call me Rosie."

A wave of emotion rose up in Crosby, *Rosie, she's called Rosie.* A silent tear rolled down his cheek and he hoped that she did not notice.

To read more by Craig Hopper, turn the page to read
the prologue of his novel

THE INSURANCE MAN

A tale of despair, friendship and love

PROLOGUE

London - 4:30pm Friday 25th June 2010

The young Personal Assistant behind the glass-topped desk put the telephone down and looked over at Blowers, who was sitting and thumbing through a home and lifestyle magazine. She smiled and said loudly, "Mr. Fitch will see you now."

Blowers noticed that she had dimples when she smiled. He smiled back and rose from the soft, leather sofa. He fastened the middle button of his suit jacket and smiled again at the young woman.

"This way," she indicated with her left hand as she rose behind her desk.

Blowers noticed that she had long, slender fingers, perfectly manicured fingernails and was not wearing an engagement or wedding ring.

The Personal Assistant stepped from behind the desk and began walking down the soft, carpeted corridor towards some deep red mahogany double doors. She was tall and slender, and Blowers guessed that she was five feet seven inches tall without the two-inch heels she was wearing. He followed two steps behind and watched how the grey, tight, hugging pencil skirt made the young woman take short steps and gave her a wiggle as she walked. A woman who looks after herself and has exquisite taste, Blowers thought to himself.

She stopped at the doors, knocked twice and then pushed them both open. "Please," she again indicated with her left hand for Blowers to enter the office.

Blowers smiled and said, "Thank you," and he entered the office of Albert Fitch, CEO of Fitch Specialty Insurance.

"You're welcome," and she winked at him.

"Now now Jenny, stop flirting with Mr. Blowers and please reschedule all my remaining meetings for today. Thank you," Fitch said with a slight hint of a Welsh accent from behind his antique mahogany desk.

The assistant nodded, "Of course Mr. Fitch."

Blowers winked at the young woman and she smiled as she closed the doors behind her. He felt the deep pile of the carpet under his feet and he looked around the office. He was impressed by its decadence; old paintings hung on the wall, a china dinner service in the rosewood cabinet, sporting trophies on the shelf.

Fitch watched Blowers and waved his hand around the room. "Just a few trinkets I've picked up from here and there." He pointed at the high-backed leather chair just to the right of his desk, "Please sit Mr. Blowers."

Blowers stepped over to the chair, leaned over the desk and offered his right hand for a handshake.

Fitch stood, fastened the middle button of his suit jacket and firmly shook the offered hand.

Blowers noticed the diamond encrusted ring on Fitch's right wedding finger.

Fitch caught Blowers glance at the wedding ring and explained, "I'm Orthodox Christian." He again indicated to the chair, "Please sit Mr. Blowers."

Blowers unbuttoned his suit jacket and sat. He sank into the soft leather and immediately felt comfortable.

Fitch immediately got down to business, "When you telephoned this morning, my assistant said that you were most insistent to speak with me this afternoon. Have you got some good news for me Mr. Blowers?"

Blowers reached into his right inside jacket pocket, pulled out a long, slender, black velvet necklace box and handed it to Fitch.

Fitch turned the box over in his hands, opened it, smiled and then snapped it shut. He put the box down on the red, leather, writing mat in front of him, leaned back in his chair and smiled. "The DeMartin diamonds. We were about to pay out for their loss."

Blowers nodded, "I believe you were."

Fitch leaned forward and tapped the necklace box with his right index finger. "How did you find them?"

Blowers reached again into his right inside jacket pocket and pulled out a photograph. He handed it to Fitch. "That photograph was taken at a charity dinner in San Francisco for US veteran soldiers a week ago. The lady on the right in the midnight blue dress is my wife and on her right…"

Fitch cut in and finished the sentence. "And on her right, is Madame Isabella DeMartin wearing the diamonds she claimed were stolen."

"Yes" Blowers confirmed, "She's not a very bright lady."

Fitch looked at Blowers and then again at the photograph. "You're married to Faith Roberts, the supermodel?"

"Yes." Blowers smiled. He could see that Fitch was impressed.

Fitch handed the photograph back to Blowers. "You're a lucky man," he grinned. He continued, "How did you come about the necklace?"

"Legally," Blowers confirmed. "And Madame DeMartin understands that in exchange for her not being prosecuted for insurance fraud, that you will keep the necklace."

Fitch was pleased and slapped the desk. "Quite so," he said loudly.

Blowers stood up and fastened the middle button of his suit jacket. "I think our business is concluded Mr. Fitch," and he took out a card from his breast pocket. "Fifty- thousand pounds into the bank account on the card if you please."

Fitch took the card but did not look at it. He held out his right hand. "Our business is indeed concluded Mr. Blowers."

Blowers firmly shook Fitch's hand, turned and walked towards the mahogany double doors. They opened before he reached them and he smiled at Fitch's Personal Assistant as he walked through. "Good day miss," he said happily.

She smiled back. "Have a nice evening Mr. Blowers."

Blowers began whistling 'happy days are here again' as he walked down the corridor towards the lifts to leave Fitch's offices.

Printed in Poland
by Amazon Fulfillment
Poland Sp. z o.o., Wrocław

54518597R00145